"The Gatekeeper"

And
Other Stories

Jeffrey Kelley

Experiment Five Media

Published by:

Experiment Five Media

Saint John, New Brunswick, Canada

First published in Canada

Archived with the Library and Archives of Canada

Catalogued Editions

Paperback: ISBN: 978-0-9951907-4-0

Edited by: Christian Crouse

For Generation X, the Forgotten Generation, not lost, but ignored.

Acknowledgements:

The Gatekeeper And Other Stories would not have been realized without the efforts and support of my fellow academic outlaw, and friend, Christian Crouse, who went above and beyond. Many thanks.

CONTENTS:

THE FOREWORD

THE STORIES

FOREWORD

Back in the day when we were fellow academic rebels, railing against the bureaucratic morass that was the university establishment and fighting to maintain our own creative independent spirits in a scholarly tradition that was being murdered by postmodern theory and Oprah's Book of the Month Club, I learned one very crucial tip in dealing with my friend, Jeff Kelley: if you weren't in the mood to have your mind bent by a dizzying array of mental acrobatics, do not ask him his opinion on something.

It wasn't that his opinions were not welcome. On the contrary, if you wanted something stripped to its bare minimalism - no matter how politically incorrect the essential might turn out to be - you simply asked Jeff. However, if you weren't mentally prepared for the labyrinthine process of deconstruction that you would have to work through in taking in his take on things, you could be left lying helpless on a cerebral cortex side road, feeling you had just been wiped out by an alpha hit-and-run.

When you were ready to receive, however, his ability to get to the heart of the matter was what made his ride to truth interesting. The methods to his madness weren't for everyone, but even his most ignorant detractors had to admit that when all was said and done, he made them see a side of things that they had missed or didn't consider - or didn't want to see. The biggest hurdle to accepting Jeff's viewpoint was the stripping down of the seemingly complex to something extraordinarily simple; people tend to want life to be much more complicated than it is, as if the mystery and miracle of its simplicities aren't profound enough.

There was one time, however, when Jeff did not give his opinion. It was a few days after September 11th, 2001, and Jeff and I were walking down the corridors of campus while I was rambling on about the horrors we all were having trouble digesting as image upon image was being shoved down our throats without mercy by a new global media gone wild. I suddenly realized that Jeff was not saying a word - which was unusual to say the least. I asked him what he was thinking, and he simply replied (and I paraphrase): "I don't have an opinion. I haven't had time to think about it." He added (and this I do not paraphrase):"It's too big."

Those three words stuck in my head for years. What may have seemed like a cop-out to the billions who were giving sustenance to a then-burgeoning Brave New Media with its 24/7 quota of talk-talk-talk, giving a mindless array of *whys, whats, whos,* and *hows,* Jeff chose the opposite route and remained silent - which was unusual to say the least. No mental acrobatics, no death-defying leaps of brain sport, no neuro-electric rollercoaster rides - just one of the most epic acts of unimaginable horror witnessed by the modern world on an unprecedented collective scale reduced to its rawest, most simplistic essentialism: it was "too big".

And it was - too big for a generation brought up on *Coca-Cola* fantasies and MTV wet dreams, where grunge rock was the biggest threat to pop our Hip Hop bubbles, and Madonna the biggest menace to our suburban chimeras. "It's too big" connotes a betrayal of all things that sustained a shared belief system inherited by the previous generation: all those quirky Hollywood endings, tension-relieving commercial breaks, and three minutes of freedom condensed in looping bubble-gum melodies. After Sept 11th, conspiracy theories that were only native to the shadows of the fringe found a whole new place in the daylight at the center of things; everything could be a lie: fathers betrayed sons, heroes became killers, and the guy sometimes didn't get the girl in the end. A new communal bond united those of a generation marked with a bulls-eye "X" with its Baby Boomer predecessors, that of a shared Post-Traumatic Syndrome Disorder, clinically undiagnosed and recklessly left untreated, to be passed on to succeeding generations while post-apocalypse has been reduced to a footnote in a refurbished form of Reality-TV history in a bid to Keep Calm and Carry On.

I am convinced that the author of the short stories presented in this collection is the same undergrad who refused to explain a world turning point in mass hyperbole and frenzied rhetoric. Since then, the mental trapeze artist has walked the tight rope many times – and fallen and got back up many times – but has now sobered up from the adrenaline addiction and sees things for what they really are in their most simplistic terms. It's a different world from pre-turn regular life: there are heroes who fall and won't get back up; there are nice guys who are going to be bad; and there are bad guys who are going to survive.

Like his hero Hemingway, Jeff writes best when he deals with men – men dealing with other men and dealing with being a man in a man's world. Misogyny is not the standard, however; the women who do appear in these stories are not bitches, whores or goddesses. They are reluctant – and bewildered – observers of male drama, pushed out of the framework by the hero's internal struggles, for there is no room for anyone else in the male psyche but his own fight with himself. In the title story "The Gatekeeper", a boxer's biggest opponent is revealed to be himself, for one more fight could surely kill him, yet he is unable to fully grasp the reality that his dream died a long time ago and he is, in fact, at death's door. In fact, all of Jeff's male characters are at death's door in some fashion – at times, figuratively; most of the time, literally. In all of them, a dream has died and taken the dreamer down with it.

Unlike the Hemingway Code Hero rising from the ashes of WWI, Jeff's heroes are all suffering from a kind of collective PTSD sorting out the internal carnage of a lost generation, defeated by an undefined betrayal of some kind – something "too big" to explain - that happened along the way in their bid to be their "own man" ... as the old saying goes: "the road to hell is paved with good intentions". These "anti-heroes" are victims of their own generational male code, betrayed by their own best intentions; the promised legends and the guaranteed myths of prelapsarian post-adolescence have led them down a wayward road that has ended in disappointment. Seamus the boxer of the pugilist portrait "The Gatekeeper" is no Rocky Balboa, but a broken man-child; the eponymous 70's-style detective of "Rourke" is no Jim Rockford, but an empty shell of a man; death row inmate Louis the Fourteenth of the prison drama "Roll on Three" is just as much a victim as the people he has killed; and in that ode to Hemingway, "Ironically, Paris", the unnamed romantic sitting in a Parisian airport bar – dreaming like Hemingway, drinking like Hemingway – is, in sobering truth, just another victim of love's timeless fiction. The source of this gallery of inner conflict is just as inexplicable as the riddle of something "too big" that defies articulation.

The unanswered question and unquestionable answer of "it's too big" connotes a shock and awe of looking into the abyss and seeing something that turns everything upside down, revealing nothingness in everything and everything as nothingness. The scream of the observer is stifled. That internal scream can be heard in all of these stories: in the over-stressed body of a relatively young boxer who has taken too many hits to the head; in a gravedigger who fears being buried alive; in the heart of a man who resigns himself to the loss of his romantic dream in Paris' City of Love. It can be heard in the alcoholic haze of a cop quietly sitting alone on his sofa, and it is vocalized in a death-row inmate's pathetic sobs as he faces his mortality in the last hours of his life. But nowhere is Edvard Munch's silent screamer discerned more than in the deceptively simple character study "Always", heard in the OCD patterns of a man who has learned he is dying and spends his remaining days sitting alone in the park, caught in a repetitive skip in a brain stuck in its groove. True carnage is not what is done externally, for that can be fixed.

Jeff's heroes are all stuck in a brain groove, "locked in, *terminal*" like the veteran detective of "Rourke" whose career stopped rising mid-way through because of a creeping feeling of futility. They are trapped in a self-contained time warp. These are stories of another time, with no cellphones, no laptops, social media, or any trace of post-Sept 11th modern technology. Time in the mid-turn has come to a standstill, capturing these men in a state of perpetual limbo, leaving them to wait things out in purgatorial part-ways: two captives held hostage in a cabin in the middle of nowhere are caught between life or death; condemned criminals question the absurdities of life while waiting to walk the mile to their execution; a man waiting in an airport bar for his plane to start boarding closes a chapter of his life because his future has dissolved; and yet another lost soul in yet another bar searching for some kind of answer in the "warm wet circles" left by the ring of his half-empty glass on the counter, forever elusive in their completeness evaporating against his own private spiraling cycle of self-destructive behavior. That thematic intermediate state of oblivion is played out in the very framework of "Dirt Road Dead", Jeff's homage to Poe in the style of a 70s Hammer film, in which a cemetery's end-of-the-road solitude acts as a divide between this world and the underworld in the mythic mindset of a dead-eyed gravedigger who sold his soul a long time ago.

Death continually invades the stories of *The Gatekeeper*. There are the death of dreams, and then there is the stuff of nightmares: in the espionage thriller "Frozen Trade", death is the ultimate threat in a fever-pitch game of survival of the fittest; in "Dirt Road Dead", it is cooled down to bone-chilling economics; in "Roll on Three", it is the gaping maw at the end of an assembly line. Then, in "Always", it is stripped down to its lowest denominator: death just happens because it is a part of life. The "too bigness" of death – the everything that is nothingness and the nothingness that is everything – has been worked out to be the simple matter that it really is. Death *is* simple; it is life that is hard, as the boxer of "The Gatekeeper" could attest to if he hadn't taken so many hits to the head and scrambled his brain.

To the Canadian readers educated on the American Dream, the lack of a Hollywood ending to these tales may disappoint, but it should be pointed out that there is hope creeping through the cracks of these trapped-in-moments-of-time stories of fragmented men. The collection is, in fact, bookended with two of the most hopeful stories offered by the author: the opening story "The Gatekeeper" ends on a melancholic note in its bittersweet innocence, while the last story "A Friendly Conversation" begins with a man confronting his past in a bid to let go of it and move on. Humanity in all its multi-faceted simplicities shines through all these stories, whether it is through a shattered heart, a scrambled brain, a dying body, or a lost soul – even cold-blooded killers shine a light of humanity in their moments of darkness. No matter how corruptible or fractured humanity is, it still endures, which may be the lesson learned after the trauma of the "too bigness" will eventually subside.

That same sense of hope peeking out from behind a blanket of bleakness belongs to a long tradition in Canadian literature, where the bigger picture pales in comparison to the little things, which are usually much more profound in their stark naked simplicity, no matter how dark, disappointing or despairing. The true mind-benders are not what is hidden, but is what is out in full view for all to see; the real puzzles don't need to be pieced together. The secret to the short stories of *The Gatekeeper* is that sometimes the *whys, whos, whats* and *hows* are not well-kept secrets at all; sometimes things are exactly what they appear to be and it doesn't make them any less profound.

And now, ladies and gentleman – Boomers, X, Y and Z's and ad infinitums - let's go on with our show …

Christian Crouse

The Gatekeeper

It would be nearly impossible to look at Seamus in those moments at the end of his career and not see a broken man sitting there, alone in a dark boxing ring with a blood-stained canvas, his body slouched on an old, wobbly, wooden stool in an empty corner, seemingly looking at his well-taped but very broken hands, while, in reality, staring deep into the nothingness that was once a promising future for one of the most gifted boxers the sport had ever known.

High above the stool, receded into the arena rafters, were large and powerful lights, most of which were turned off now; one of the lights that remained lit was burning down directly atop of Seamus, and the harsh shadows created by that lone light seemed to haunt his face.

As he approached the ring, Bruce finally began to accept that he had let Seamus go one round too many for his own profit; Seamus was, in many ways, gone, and he would never fully return. Bruce paused as he arrived at the bottom of the ring steps. He rubbed his forehead and looked down; he was perhaps the closest he had ever come to feeling empathy - or remorse. He rubbed the back of his neck with his right hand and looked down at the boxing robe he had laid across his left forearm; next, he sighed, and then climbed up the steps and slipped through the ropes into the ring.

Bruce approached Seamus and, squatting down onto his haunches, he looked into Seamus' eyes. He could see they were focused on the imperceptible distance of the boxer's life's journey - and its failures, all which lay within the cracks and chips and tears of bone and ligament below the skin surface of his crippled hands. After a moment - mere seconds that felt like an eternity stretching into the oblivion of shattered dreams - Bruce spoke: "You in there, Seamus?"

He held his breath not knowing if Seamus would, or

even could, respond.

"I ain't never laid down for nobody, Bruce," Seamus said, "Never."

"I know, Seamus," Bruce said, "I know."

"We could have made a lot of money, and my hands ... I would still have my hands ... but I didn't do it, Bruce, I ain't never laid down."

"I know, Seamus, and I am very proud of you for that," Bruce lied.

"We had more offers than I remember, for a lot of cash. More than any champ was ever offered," Seamus said as he continued to stare into the oblivion.

"Everyone wanted to get past the gatekeeper. It would have made careers for those fighters. It would have set us up," Bruce admitted.

"But I ain't never rolled over, not for nobody," Seamus repeated.

"And you should be very proud of that," Bruce said, quietly blaming Seamus' morality for both the fighter's obvious brain trauma and his own thin bank account.

Bruce took a deep breath and stood up. He draped Seamus' robe over the boxer's bare shoulders, then put his hand down on one of them for a moment, relieved his friend was at least now talking. But he was worried this was the last fight, and last payday, they would ever have together.

Bruce removed his hand from Seamus' shoulder and turned away. He began to walk to the ropes when Seamus spoke words that brought Bruce to a halt.

"Think she'll come tonight, Bruce?" Seamus asked.

Bruce felt a chill run through his body.

"Seamus …?" he queried.

"Brooke, do you think Brooke will come to watch me fight tonight?"

"Seamus …" Bruce replied, "I'm not sure what you're getting at here …"

"Brooke," Seamus repeated. "She wants me to stop, says I'm getting all scrambled up. She said she don't wanna watch me fight no more, doesn't want to watch me get …

scrambled-up. Do you think she'll come?"

Bruce silently cursed his sudden unwanted emergence of guilt, and looked past Seamus, down the aisle to the access to the arena the boxers use; as he did, he saw Brooke emerge through the fighters' entrance. It was the first time in years he had laid eyes on her.

"Yea, Seamus," Bruce finally answered, looking across at Brooke, "I think she'll come."

Bruce exited the ring and began the path towards her, while Seamus just stared downcast through his once powerful hands and into oblivion.

Brooke watched silently as Bruce came nearer; she knew something was wrong with Seamus, or Bruce would never have called her. She could tell just by looking at the once proud fighter, now slumped on a stool in the empty ring, that something had finally been scrambled, that he had gone the distance one too many times, and this time he did not make it back; now the cruelest of fates was coming to collect a toll for the gifts Seamus had over-used.

"What's wrong with him?" Brooke asked Bruce when he finally arrived at her end of the aisle; she already damned well knew what was wrong with Seamus, and she blamed Bruce.

"He's out far more often than he's in now," Bruce replied. He felt something as he spoke, something he had never felt before, and when he looked at Brooke, he realized it was shame. "Brooke, you need to get him out of the ring."

"I'll try," Brooke said crisply, coldly.

As she walked down the aisle, she changed from rigid to sad, then became somewhat fearful. When she reached the steps, she stifled back a few tears and then climbed up into the ring. She took a deep breath, forced on a smile that only ended up looking sad, and approached Seamus much the same way Bruce had, squatting down in front of him and looking him in the eyes, trying very hard not to let her smile land on the canvas by fighting through the pain in her heart.

"Hey there, slugger," Brooke said with a slight catch in her throat; she had not seen Seamus in years, and now that she had, she realized he looked the same, only broken.

"Slugger is for baseball players, Brooke," Seamus said, lifting his head to lay his eyes on her, and he smiled, genuinely, fully, and happily, and it broke Brooke's heart. "I'm a boxer."

"Well, I like slugger for you, because you are always slugging away against all odds."

"I'm the Irish Thunder," Seamus said with pride.

"I prefer slugger," Brooke said, fighting hard to keep her smile.

"I know you don't want me to fight no more, Brooke," Seamus began.

"Seamus ... I ... we ..." Brooke stammered, but Seamus cut her off.

"I'm gonna quit. Win or lose, this – tonight - is gonna be my last fight."

"But Seamus ..." Brooke began.

"I can beat him, Brooke. I can beat this guy. I'm going to leave him right in the middle of the ring and then we can go home. I ain't even bringing my gloves home, I'm gonna leave 'em right here in the ring too."

Unsure of what she could say, Brooke stood up and began to climb out of the ring.

"I ain't never laid down for nobody, Brooke. Not once. Not ever," Seamus called after her with pride.

"I know, Seamus, I know," Brooke replied without looking back, fighting off her tears.

Brooke began to walk back up the aisle towards Bruce, with her sorrow turning to anger, blaming Bruce more and more for allowing Seamus to fight this long after so many gloves had taken new pieces out of him every time he fought.

When she arrived at the top of the aisle to the arena entrance, Brooke came face-to-face with Bruce and looked at him with disdain. "How long has he been like this?" she demanded.

"Brooke, he was drifting long before you threw him out."

"He was never this bad," she stated with certainty.

"He was closer than you realized, but worse since you

threw him out," Bruce admitted. "But he was always much worse than you wanted to admit to yourself."

"You just sat here and watched while he scrambled his brain. You're responsible for this. He trusted you to look out for him. You're a real bastard, Bruce," Brooke condemned.

Challenged, Bruce became defensive.

"He was never going to stop fighting. *You* left him, but I was right here. I was here for Seamus. Where the hell were *you?*!"

"You enabled him, you coward."

For several eternal moments they stood in silence, then Brooke spoke again.

"I think he's worried I'll think he took a dive tonight."

"Why do you think that?" Bruce asked her.

"He wanted me to know he never laid down for anyone. I guess he wants me to know he lost honestly."

"Brooke," Bruce said earnestly, "Seamus *won* tonight."

Seamus was warming up for the fight. He was loose, and his body looked very much like a fighter in his prime despite the fact he was now in his forties. Physically, it seemed as though time had forgotten Seamus in his twenties, or early thirties, but for every great blessing, there is a terrible curse.

Bruce was holding the pads and he was warming up Seamus, just as he had done for every fight Seamus had for over twenty years. Their partnership had outlasted the grunge rock movement, two Iraqi wars, and most marriages.

"I can beat this guy, Bruce," Seamus said with confidence.

"There ain't a man walking the earth you can't knock out with those hands of yours, Irish Thunder," Bruce replied. He watched Seamus as he moved the pads about a little; particularly, he was watching Seamus' eyes, and he thought they were looking just a bit glassy.

"Ever regret sticking with me, Bruce?" Seamus asked his

coach.

"Not ever. Not for one single minute," Bruce replied.

"I've never been more than a gatekeeper. Never even had a title shot. You could have made more money with someone else, Bruce," Seamus said.

"You are not a gatekeeper, Seamus - you are *the* gatekeeper. You are the most feared man in boxing. Every single guy that got by you became the world champ. And there were not too many of them."

"I ain't never laid down, Bruce."

"I know, and I respect that," the coach said without conviction.

"You could have been riding in a caddy, and I wouldn't be living in a shoe box," Seamus said regretfully.

"You never could have lived with yourself," Bruce stated matter-of-factly. He put the pads down and sat in a chair, and Seamus sat in the chair opposite him and held out his hands. He began checking the tape on the boxer's hands one last time.

"Think she'll come tonight, Bruce?" Seamus asked.

"Seamus, Brooke's not coming," Bruce said flatly.

"She said she can't watch it no more … that I am getting all scrambled, ya know."

"I know, Seamus."

"I love her, Bruce, but this is who I am. I don't know nothing else."

Bruce watched Seamus' eyes as they grew more and more glassy.

"Seamus, when was the last time you spoke to Brooke?" he asked.

"I don't know," Seamus said, straining to remember. "It must have been before I left home, to come to the arena."

"Seamus, listen to me very carefully. You have not lived with Brooke in over five years," Bruce said, coaching Seamus on how to remember.

"In … five …" the boxer slowly processed.

"Seamus, are you alright?"

"Oh yeah," Seamus lied. "I was just fooling around, you

know … sort of wishful thinking."

There was a knock at the door and it opened before any invitation to enter had been offered. The fight doctor entered, smelling of gin and looking like he had not seen the inside of a shower in days. Bruce stood up while the doctor took his place in the chair opposite Seamus and began to examine the fighter.

"How is the Thunder feeling?" the doctor asked the boxer.

"Real loose doc, real loose," Seamus spoke with the confidence of a man half his age. "I got this guy in five rounds tops."

"He's a tough kid, Seamus, just like you were coming up. He might take you the distance," the fight doctor said.

"Never gonna happen," Seamus replied. "Say doc, think Brooke will come to see me fight tonight?"

"Why would she do that?" the doctor asked inattentively.

"Well, I know she don't want me fighting no more, but I

always fight better when she's here."

"Seamus," the fight doctor said, "you know you and Brooke broke up, right?"

""Er, yeah …" Seamus said, struggling to remember. "About three, five years ago, but I just thought it would be nice if she was here, ya know. Just wishful thinking, doc."

"Well, you are good to go, Thunder," the fight doctor said as he stood up. The doctor moved to the door and motioned to Bruce to step out into the hall with him, then disappeared out of the locker room.

"I'll be right out here, Seamus. You stay loose," he instructed the fighter.

"You got it, Bruce," Seamus said; he got to his feet and began to pace and rotate his shoulders as Bruce ducked into the hallway.

Outside, Bruce found the doctor standing beside a bank of pay phones, something else that was quickly fading away and becoming as obsolete as the fighter in the locker room. Bruce looked up at the fight doctor, who pulled a flask of gin from his coat and took a sip before speaking.

"He's getting worse, Bruce. I can't clear him next time. If we ever got caught, I'd lose my license."

The doctor put his flask back in his coat pocket, then turned and wobbled off.

Once the fight doctor was out of sight, Bruce stared long and hard at the bank of pay phones outside the locker room, then after the agony of reflection, he began to sort through his pockets for some change.

. . . .

"You knew he was like this, and let him fight?!"

Brooke's anger was apparent in her voice.

"He was going to fight anyway," Bruce countered.

As they argued, neither Brooke nor Bruce had noticed that Seamus had risen from his stool, and with the difficulty of an eager toddler or a confused old man, he had stumbled through the ring ropes and he was making his way down the aisle towards them.

"You were his coach – and his friend. You were supposed to protect him."

"From what? You hurt him more than boxing ever did," Bruce claimed.

"The hell I did," an insulted Brooke replied.

"You did. Seamus only ever loved two things: you and boxing. Well, after you threw him out on the streets, all he had was boxing. Your tough love was one hell of a beat down."

"I wasn't going to watch him die in that ring," Brooke replied.

Brooke and Bruce were staring each other down when they both noticed Seamus' shadow. They each turned to look at the fighter as he stood over them, physically unimposing, no longer the man he had once been.

"Brooke, did you come to see me fight?" Seamus asked.

"No, I missed it, Slugger," Brooke said, fighting back tears. "I can't watch you hurt yourself anymore."

"I won, Brooke. I beat him. In the first minute of the fifth round."

"I heard, Seamus," Brooke replied, with a catch in her voice.

"Brooke ..." Seamus began.

"Yes?"

"I don't wanna fight no more."

"I am so glad to hear that, Seamus. I am very proud of you for that," she replied, tears beginning to run down her face.

"Brooke ..." Seamus said again.

"Yes?"

"Can I come home?"

"Yes."

Brooke let her tears fall freely now, and helped Seamus along as the three of them - the fighter, *her* lover, and the trainer - left the arena, and the sport of boxing, behind them.

Left in the ring were Seamus' boxing gloves.

Frozen Trade

It was 1971.

It was behind the Iron Curtain, inside the Soviet Union.

It was a desolate place.

It was winter.

It was cold. It was very, very, cold.

They were inside a small log cabin. The cabin was far from livable; a bitter wind howled through the walls of the structure, and it sounded like a wounded animal, carrying with it snow, desperation, and death. It may well have been colder inside the cabin than outside in the unrelenting Russian winter; it may have been even colder in the cabin than it was in the bitter war between the Soviet Union and the United States of America.

There were two men in the cabin, and they were captives. The men were Smith and O'Brien, and there was nothing outwardly remarkable about either of them. Both men shopped off the rack; both were around, or just over, average height and weight; both could blend in and disappear into almost any crowd of people in almost any place in the world. Smith and O'Brien were not easy men to notice.

They were tied to very old solid wooden chairs that creaked loudly and desperately under their weight. The chairs were so uncomfortable that it was doubtful the manufacturer had actually intended anyone to sit in them for any great length of time.

Smith and O'Brien's wrists and ankles were lashed to the ancient chairs, and black hoods covered their heads, blocking out all light. Both men had been robbed of their coats, gloves, and scarves, and they sat there, shivering, in nothing more than dress shoes, slacks, and dress shirts.

It was cold.

It was torture.

Smith and O'Brien were shivering so hard that their bindings were cutting into their skin. As they shivered and bled, the two men heard the door to the cabin open, followed by the hard sounds of deliberate footsteps. Two new men entered the cabin, both as cold and unforgiving as the Soviet Tundra, both KGB agents trained in counter-espionage, both cunning, and both ruthless.

Pavlov was the senior of the two KGB operatives, and he entered the cabin first; Volkov, his right hand, entered the cabin second and closed the door behind him.

The two Soviets were well dressed for the winter, with long coats, gloves, and Ushanka hats. They were relatively comfortable in the crushing cold that was cruelly assaulting Smith and O'Brien.

The cabin was very sparse. There were two empty chairs facing those occupied by Smith and O'Brien, a Soviet flag, a wall clock, and a table; on the table there was a bottle of Vodka and two glasses. Pavlov walked directly to one chair and sat down; Volkov walked to the table, flipped over the glasses, opened the vodka, and prepared two drinks. He passed one drink to Pavlov, who then raised it to his comrade.

"Spasiva," Pavlov's icy voice toasted, cutting crisply through the cold, causing both Smith and O'Brien to stiffen.

"Nostravia," Volkov replied, saluting Pavlov with his glass, then both men drank their vodka with the stiff rigor of soldiers.

After they had downed their shots, Pavlov passed his glass to Volkov, who returned both glasses to the table, then walked over to the prisoners and stood between them; once in position, Volkov looked at Pavlov. Pavlov removed his hat, and then nodded to Volkov, who in turn reached out, grabbed both hoods, and viciously pulled them off of the captives with a single swift movement of each arm.

As Smith and O'Brien struggled to force their eyes to adjust to the light while their bodies continued their involuntary shivering, Pavlov leaned back in his chair to create the opposing image of comfort in the sub-zero temperature. He removed his gloves, not just purely as a visual cue, but as a psychological trick. He looked intently at the two westerners. Finally, in broken English, Pavlov spoke:

"Is 8:45 in the morning of the 10th day of February when your country changes everything."

It was O'Brien who answered Pavlov, his impertinent voice cracked dry, and thick with an Irish accent: "Now exactly whose country are you talking about here, lad?"

After O'Brien spoke, Pavlov nodded to Volkov, and Volkov slapped O'Brien hard across the back of his head, pitching him forward to the limit of his restraints. After a moment, O'Brien righted himself as best he could in his chair and Pavlov resumed speaking, calmly, crisply.

"I continue. 1962 we make trade of human assets. Two of your captured spies for our ... detained comrade. After this, we have certain trust."

"Except we don't trust you. That's why we have spies." This time it was Smith who interrupted, with contempt in his voice.

"Then what name," Pavlov replied, "would you give this ... *arrangement?*"

"This is a card game," Smith said sharply, "and all hands are on the felt. The first time one of us lifts his palm off the felt - well, there will be no going back."

Pavlov smiled, put his gloves back on, stood up, and responded coolly: "In Soviet Union, Mr. Smith, we do not play old maid. We play chess and you are nothing more than pawns. Question is, will your Uncle Sam sacrifice you in gambit?"

After he finished speaking, Pavlov nodded to Volkov, who then put the hoods back over the heads of the prisoners while Pavlov replaced his hat on his own head. The prisoners could hear the sounds of the Soviets' footsteps, accented by the howling wind, as they walked to the door, opened it, and exited into the hostile climate.

. . . .

Neither Smith nor O'Brien were aware of how much time had passed since the Soviets had left the cabin. It felt as though it had been a very long time, but it was impossible to tell for sure; eventually, however, they again heard the cabin door open and the Soviets enter.

Pavlov and Volkov came into the room in the same fashion as before: Pavlov first, followed by Volkov. Pavlov went directly to his chair, sat down, and removed his hat; Volkov walked deeper into the cabin, and took his place standing between the two prisoners. When Pavlov nodded, Volkov again viciously pulled the hoods off the westerners, snapping back their heads; he looked to Pavlov, and Pavlov nodded.

Taking his cue, Volkov walked to the table and poured two large vodkas; as he did, Pavlov stared hard at the hostages with disinterest and disdain.

Volkov again passed one glass to him, who accepted while continuing to fix his icy gaze on the two sitting in front of him.

"Spasiva," Pavlov toasted again.

"Nostravia," Volkov again replied. And again, the two Soviets downed their vodkas stiffly, and again, Pavlov passed his glass to Volkov, and again, Volkov returned the glasses to the table before taking his place in the empty chair beside his superior.

Pavlov remained silent as the wind continued to howl through the cabin. After a chilling, unnerving few moments, finally Pavlov spoke.

"Vodka," he said, "is the only salvation of Soviet winter."

"You really ought to try whiskey, lad," O'Brien returned in his cracked, thick Irish accent.

"Hmm," Pavlov mocked O'Brien dryly. "I will stay with Vodka. Is a good drink... strong, like Mother Russia."

Pavlov changed his focus from O'Brien to Smith. He sniffed the air, and his lips and nostrils curled, and then he turned his head to address his comrade.

"The aroma in here speaks for itself."

Volkov made a snort of derision by way of reply. The westerners had been in the cabin for a very long time, and they had never been given a bathroom break, and with this simple trick, the Soviets had robbed Smith and O'Brien of their dignity.

With the slightest of smiles, Pavlov returned his focus to them, leaned back in his chair, and spoke with authority in his fragmented English: "His name – Volkov, which means the *wolf*. It suits him I think. My name, Pavlov."

"What does Pavlov mean?" Smith asked.

"To you," Pavlov replied, "it shall mean last and only hope." He took a pause and then resumed. "In this game of chess, you are nothing but pawns of America, but Volkov and I, we are knights of Soviet Union."

"I'm an Irishman," O'Brien interrupted.

"You do not fool us," Pavlov replied with amusement, "we know that you too are American spy."

"Oh, I may be a lot of things, lad, but I can assure you there are three things I am not," O'Brien retorted.

"And what three things are these?" Pavlov asked.

"A protestant, a virgin, or a damned Yankee," O'Brien snarled in his Irish accent.

"But you are a liar," Pavlov stated.

"Aye, most times," O'Brien agreed.

"What do you think of this one, Volkov?" Pavlov asked his comrade.

"I think Ireland has nothing. He needs to make himself American for trade," the wolf responded.

"Yes, I think same," Pavlov agreed. "And what do *you* think, Mr. Smith?"

"I think I made a poor career choice," Smith quipped.

"Funny, Smith," Pavlov replied. "But I want to know what you think of your comrade."

"Not much," Smith admitted, adding, "and I cannot stress this enough, we are *not* together."

"But yet, you are both here in the company of Comrade Volkov and myself."

Pavlov smiled, taking delight in his victory in their battle of wits. Then, after his celebratory pause, he continued: "In 1962, when spies were traded on checkpoint Charlie Bridge in Berlin, the world changed."

"You mentioned that before," Smith said, cold and irritated.

"Yes, I did," agreed Pavlov. "But why did it change? What was reason for our new strategic directions?"

"To save lives," Smith answered.

"Volkov," Pavlov asked, "does Smith lie to me, or to himself?"

"Maybe he is not smart," Volkov replied.

Smith raised his voice: "Life may not have much value to you, but it does to us!"

"Fool," Volkov sneered.

"Ahh," Pavlov calmly re-took control. "I see now. You value life, and you choose to believe America shares your sympathies. Yes. Comrade Volkov is quite correct: you *are* fool."

Pavlov sat forward now, and leaned his elbows on his

knees to address the men more intimately.

"Mr. Smith, you and Mr. O'Brien mean nothing to your country. You are pawns for political advancement, nothing more."

"*His* country, lad," O'Brien disputed.

Pavlov ignored O'Brien and stood up. Volkov did the same. Pavlov then stepped in close to Smith and looked down.

"In war, Smith, governments do not see men, only assets," Pavlov smiled, then addressed his comrade: "Leave hoods off. They have clock to help pass time."

Pavlov turned his back to the prisoners and walked to the door, where he waited for Volkov to open it. As Volkov did, Pavlov added a last chilling remark: "…make no mistake, Smith - this is very cold war."

He stepped briskly out through the door, followed by Volkov, who closed it with chilling authority.

The wind howled as Smith spoke to O'Brien for the first time.

"Those two are real bastards," Smith observed.

"Aye, and that clock on the wall, it's not working."

O'Brien motioned towards the clock with his head, and Smith craned his neck to see that O'Brien was right: the hands on the clock were not moving.

"Time stands still in hell," Smith said.

....

The air in the cabin was growing colder, but the two prisoners were no longer shivering; hyperthermia was settling into their bodies. Death was beginning to look eminent, and as the end of their lives drew closer, O'Brien became a philosopher.

"Where are you from, Smith?" he asked.

"The United States of America," Smith replied indignantly.

"Ahh, I see," O'Brien sighed, "then you must know my cousin. His name is Patrick."

"Sorry," Smith grumbled, then realized that his curt reply was uncalled for. "Sorry, O'Brien. I'm from Sacramento."

"Is that in California?"

"Yes, it is," Smith replied.

"Is it nice in California?"

"Very," Smith admitted. "Where are you from?"

"Belfast," O'Brien replied.

"Is it nice there?" Smith asked, returning the cordiality.

"Not really," O'Brien answered, "everything keeps exploding."

"And whose fault is that, now?"

"The British," O'Brien answered.

"How do you figure?"

"Ever have a houseguest that just won't fucking leave?" O'Brien asked rhetorically.

After a moment, the two men facing hyperthermia and death began to laugh. They continued to laugh until the door to the cabin opened, and Pavlov entered, followed by Volkov.

Pavlov's return brought a sinister chill back into the

room; he walked with purpose to the table and stood there. Volkov closed the door and followed him.

Pavlov looked at the two prisoners with vicious intent as Volkov silently poured two large vodkas and passed one to Pavlov.

"Spasiva," Pavlov said to Volkov, without taking his eyes off the prisoners.

"Nostravia," Volkov replied, and then the two men stiffly drank their vodkas. It was at this point that O'Brien addressed his Soviet captors.

"Please, have a seat comrades, stay awhile," O'Brien taunted.

"Yes, please, do sit; when you stand, it makes me nervous," Smith added.

"These men, Volkov," Pavlov said, his eyes still fixed on the prisoners, "they have grown funny, don't you think."

"HET," Volkov answered in the negative.

"I think you are right," Pavlov agreed. "I think they are not funny." Pavlov methodically stepped to his chair, sat down, removed his hat, and then spoke in an eerie calm voice. "Smith, we know why you are here in Soviet Union, we draw you out like starving animal."

"You set me up," Smith said defiantly.

"Of course," Pavlov replied, "you are enemy spy." Pavlov slowly shifted his stare to O'Brien. "What we do not know is why *you*, O'Brien, are in Moscow."

"I'd have gladly told you, had you only asked," O'Brien replied.

"But if I ask, you will only lie," Pavlov countered. "Americans lie to Soviets."

"Are you suggesting," Smith responded, "that the Russians..."

"Soviets!" Volkov barked.

"Fine. Are you saying the Soviets do not lie to us?" Smith asked.

"To *you*, lad," O'Brien corrected Smith.

"Enough childish bickering," Pavlov said, as if actually speaking to children. "It is America that has damaged our strategic truces."

Pavlov then leaned back in his chair and Volkov stepped up in front of O'Brien.

"Comrade Volkov will ask you now."

Volkov leaned in towards O'Brien closely, leaving mere inches between them.

"Pretty please, Mr. O'Brien," he mocked, "why were you in Moscow?"

"For Ak-47 rifles," O'Brien replied.

"Why should you want Soviet AK-47 rifles?!" Volkov demanded.

"I'm in the Irish Republican Army, lad - we wanted them to defend ourselves from the British invaders," O'Brien answered.

"Would Smith not give you American imitations, AR-18?" Volkov pressed.

"Well, lad," O'Brien replied, "I never asked him."

Volkov stood up and looked at O'Brien a moment, then the Soviet backhanded the prisoner with great force.

Pavlov stood up slowly as O'Brien spit blood from his mouth.

"Mr. O'Brien, that is Comrade Volkov's way of saying you are liar."

Pavlov turned on his heels and walked to the door. Volkov followed him and the two Soviets left the frigid cabin, once again leaving the westerners alone.

For a few moments, Smith just stared at the door with a look of shock on his face; he had been caught off guard by O'Brien's comment.

"AK-47s? Are you serious?!" Smith snapped.

"Well, at first we planned to throw the bullets at the British, but … well, physics, lad," O'Brien replied dryly.

"Libya," Smith counseled O'Brien. "They stockpiled after World War Two."

"Well, that is information I would have loved to have had before I came to Moscow to die," O'Brien said.

"Don't worry, O'Brien, we will get out of this. They will trade for our lives," Smith said with authority.

"Maybe you will, Smith, but I am a very low level asset," O'Brien confessed.

"Listen, I'm a very senior field operative. I know too much for them not to trade for me."

Smith swelled up with pride as he spoke, and O'Brien looked at him through the corner of his eyes with judgment.

"Being in your line of work, you must have regrets, Smith. What ones haunt you?" O'Brien asked.

"Why?" Smith asked, with the natural suspicion of a trained spy entering his voice.

"You don't want to die with a heavy soul, Smith," O'Brien said.

"They will trade for us. We'll be fine," Smith said.

"And if they don't?" O'Brien asked.

After a long pause, and a deep breath, Smith answered, "The deaths ... death follows everywhere in my line of work."

"T'is dirty work," O'Brien agreed.

"And what about you, O'Brien?" Smith asked. "What

do you regret?"

"*She bid me take life easy, where the grass grows on the weirs.
But I was young and foolish, and now I am full of tears,*" O'Brien
answered, quoting Yeats.

"So a woman," Smith replied, as more of a statement
than a question.

"Aye," O'Brien said. "She left Belfast, and I stayed."

"Why?" Smith asked.

"You have your war, Smith, and I have mine."

....

Smith and O'Brien found themselves remarkably somber
after their talk, and they remained silent for some time. After
what felt like hours, their Soviet keepers returned. Pavlov
entered the room again, briskly and with more purpose than
in the past. He stopped beside the table and waited as
Volkov closed the door and walked to his side.

Keeping with custom, Volkov fixed two large vodkas

and passed a glass to Pavlov.

"Spasiva," Pavlov toasted.

"Nostravia," Volkov toasted in return, and they drank their vodkas stiffly.

Pavlov passed his glass to Volkov, who returned it to the table as Pavlov looked long and hard at Smith.

"Communications have failed!" Pavlov shouted. "Why?!"

"F-failed?" Smith stuttered, confused.

"Yes," Pavlov answered him. "Failed."

"I don't believe you," Smith stated.

"No?" Pavlov said.

"No," Smith continued. "You have an exchange all set up, and it is soon. You are just looking to squeeze information out of me now because you're running low on time. This is all jive."

"We know all there is to know about you, Smith!" Volkov barked. "This is why we were able to draw you out so easy, like child."

"Your government has made your lives forfeit," Pavlov stated matter-of-factly.

"You're a liar!" Smith yelled, with desperation seeping into his voice, as if he was questioning the trade for the first time.

"I see...." Pavlov said calmly, and then he turned to Volkov and nodded.

Volkov walked to Smith, leaned forward and with an eerily calm tone spoke a single name:

"Salvador Allende."

Volkov fell in line behind Pavlov, and the two Soviets left the cabin as briskly as they had entered.

"Salvador Allende is the president of Chile," Smith volunteered to O'Brien.

"I really don't care," O'Brien replied.

"Why is that?" Smith asked.

"Because I don't think he will trade for us either," O'Brien answered.

Smith and O'Brien were sitting in silence. They no longer shivered, and they no longer felt the cold, though it was now colder than ever. They could still hear the howling wind and see the snow blow through the walls of the cabin, so they knew they were cold, and they knew they had very little time left, for they knew if they remained exposed to these temperatures much longer they would die. As they waited for the word of salvation from the west, the door to the cabin opened and again Pavlov entered, followed by Volkov, who was carrying a manila folder; he closed the door.

"You still believe us to lie, Comrade Smith?" Pavlov asked.

"Yes, I do," Smith answered.

Pavlov looked to his companion. "Volkov," he said, "please, show Comrade Smith what is in file."

Volkov stepped up, and laid the file folder open across Smith's lap, and Smith's face betrayed him.

Looking down at the pages on his lap, Smith was unable to find his voice. The pages showed his role in the CIA's unsuccessful attempts to rig the Chilean election against Allende, and his mission parameters in Moscow to determine if the Soviets had any intent to enter trade agreements with Chile.

As Smith was focused on the papers in his lap, Pavlov addressed O'Brien.

"Salvador Allende wished improved economic agreements with Soviet Union and Cuba. Smith was sent to Moscow to discover our intentions. He is here to protect economic interests of the west."

After he finished speaking, Pavlov nodded to Volkov, who closed the file and removed it from Smith's lap. Pavlov led Volkov to the door, then turned back to look at the prisoners.

"It appears the trade has become frozen. If no exchange is offered by midnight, you shall be executed as enemies of Soviet Union."

Pavlov led his faithful companion out of the cabin, and Smith just stared at the door, unsettled, shattered. He heard O'Brien speak, but his voice seemed distant.

"They aren't coming for you, lad."

The Irish accent was fading away as he spoke, but Smith was slow to notice the change in his fellow hostage's voice.

"No, you're wrong," Smith argued, desperation in his voice. "They are working on the trade right now."

"And now why do you say that?"

O'Brien's accent was now completely gone, replaced by the accent of the American mid-west.

"Because I know too much to be left in the hands of the Russians," Smith said with agitation.

"Well now, son, that is exactly my point."

O'Brien's new voice hung in the air and Smith was hit with the perplexing realization that the man he had been sitting with all this time was not an Irishman, but an American.

While O'Brien was drinking the vodka, his mind was trying to fool his body into believing he was warm. Alcohol can do that, and it makes freezing to death a little less unpleasant.

O'Brien was sitting in Pavlov's chair now, his having been broken to pieces when he forced it back and brought all the weight down on the arm as he crashed it against the floor. Smith was dead, of course, his corpse still tied to his chair but his neck broken.

As he heard the door to the cabin open behind him, O'Brien took a long pull from the bottle of vodka and listened as the Soviets entered the room and walked directly to Smith's corpse without word or shock.

Volkov examined Smith's body, then he looked up at Pavlov and nodded, and Pavlov knew with certainty that Smith was dead.

Pavlov grabbed the chair that Volkov had used before and swung it around ninety degrees to face O'Brien, and he sat down. O'Brien passed the vodka to him and he took a drink.

"You are no Irish Republican soldier," Pavlov stated after swallowing the hard liquor; meanwhile, Volkov calmly circled the room and took a place standing behind O'Brien.

"I'm from Nebraska," O'Brien replied, reaching for the bottle.

"Is Nebraska nice place?"

"Well, it ain't no Sacramento," O'Brien replied and took a pull from the bottle, then passed it back to Pavlov.

"I see Comrade Smith was too valuable to lose," Pavlov observed as he took a drink.

"Something like that," O'Brien agreed. Behind him, Volkov began to remove his scarf and wrap his fists in either end.

"And you are - what?" Pavlov asked. "If not Irish soldier?"

"Well, comrade," O'Brien replied, "I'm *The Silencer.*"

"Is despicable job you have," Pavlov said, understanding exactly what O'Brien's job was and passing him the bottle of vodka.

"Spasiva," O'Brien said as he accepted and raised the bottle, then took a long last drink, and passed it back to Pavlov.

"Nostravia," Pavlov said as he accepted the bottle and raised it in salute; as Pavlov put the bottle to his lips, Volkov dropped his scarf around O'Brien's throat and pulled it tight, strangling him.

As Pavlov drank, O'Brien died.

Warm Wet Circles

They were warm wet circles, and he twirled the bottom of his glass over them repeatedly.

It did not take long for the circles to evaporate on a hot August night, but in December they seemed to linger longer. He had noticed the shift in the speed with which the warm wet circles evaporated night after night. The changes in the rate of evaporation marked for him the changing seasons; but whether it was autumn, winter, spring, or summer, they were still warm wet circles.

The waitress was a very pretty lady, and she looked like someone he once knew. He watched her earlier in the evening as she fought her way through the supper crowd. After the supper crowd left, she always looked as though she felt better, relieved maybe, until about an hour before the night crowd began to fill the room. They were like vultures descending on the bar room like vicious scavengers from above. When the vultures began to arrive, she always seemed to possess the spirit of impending doom.

During the lull in business, after the supper crowd and before the night vultures, she was attentive to his needs and he could often feel her eyes gazing in his direction, studying him in some way. Whenever she looked at him, she had on her face a smile masked as a frown, or maybe it was the other way around.

He looked up as she walked towards him and he held his glass in the air. He used his index finger on his free hand to point at his empty glass. She took the glass from him and he stared again at the warm wet circles that it had left behind; they were evaporating now, but he played with the condensation on the table by running his index finger over the circumference of their remains. A funny memory took hold of him, but not a funny one.

She always sighed when she collected a glass from his table of circles. The circles did not mesmerize her; she did not like them anymore than she disliked them. She felt especially bad when he stopped talking while he placed his orders. He was shy or depressed at first. Then he would flirt with her, but in a harmless manner, not like the night vultures, but it was just another transparent mask anyway. Finally, he always reached the point where he could no longer hold his head up, but just pointed. It was not intoxication as much as it was something else that forced him to avoid eye contact. She tilted the glass under the tap behind the bar to avoid a big head, and then she stood there a few moments to look at him.

The band had played a lot of songs composed of tragic stories; she always worried about him after a band did that. The band was long gone now, as was the night crowd. The band and the night crowd would be back again another night, as interchangeable as ever. She began picking up empty glasses and wiping down tables. The bus boys were putting the chairs up now.

The circles were evaporating, and they were nearly gone when her shadow crossed his table. He always paid his bill at the beginning of the next day, or afternoon as it were; there was just something about taking money from him after seeing him sit there all night that just made it too difficult for her. He put his glass down and watched as the condensation turned to warm wet circles on the table. For seven years, he had not taken a drink, not a single drop, but on the first day of the eighth year he had discovered these warm wet circles.

He never finished his last glass, not all the way anyhow. He always thought this was humorous at the end of the night. He bought the glass, he had a contract with the glass until the end, and he always left the glass half-empty. This was ironic to him; after all, he took the best part of the glass and threw the rest away, the leftover part, the part nobody would ever want. Then he always blamed himself, but he would have blamed himself just the same if the glass had walked away from him. Experience had taught him that.

He pushed his chair out and stood up; the waitress always came over when he did this. She had to unlock the door to let him out. She would always hold the door as he squeezed by her and stepped out. He would always pause here and turn towards her and put on his hat, and then he would always say the same thing, "I think what I miss most are the warm wet circles." He always gave her a nervous laugh here with a slightly forced smile. As he turned, she always told him to have a good night; she did the same thing this time.

When she went back in to the bar, she picked up his empty glass, the bus boys had missed it, and it was then that she noticed the warm wet circles. She thought about the only words he ever spoke at the end of the night as she watched the warm wet circles evaporate. She understood now why he came.

She also laughed sadly.

Dirt Road Dead

The ferryman carries souls to the underworld.

In Greek mythology, Charon ferries the souls of the dead across the river Styx and the river Acheron, the waters that separate the world of the dead, the Underworld, from the world of the living, but Charon requires that the departed pay a toll before he will ferry them, and those who die without the fare, or who are not buried with sufficient funds to book passage upon their deaths, are cursed to wander the banks of the river Styx for eternity.

To most, this is mythology, just a story and nothing more, but Cooper always took heed of it, and every time he buried a body, both those bodies he murdered and those that had been by murdered by others and then brought to him to lay low in the earth, he made certain to leave two pennies on their eyes to pay Charon: two pennies for the toll.

Cooper was a gravedigger, and he was not a traditionally religious man in the context of any one religion, but he did believe that there was a hell waiting for him after the life he had lived and all of his wicked deeds, and the only possible salvation he might have, his only bargaining chip, was that he never left a soul trapped to wandering the shores of the river Styx. It was not much to barter with after the way he had lived, but Cooper had always been a desperate man with desperate demons.

Mr. Coachman was a different case; he had no spiritual beliefs. For Mr. Coachman, there was no crossing rivers to the Underworld, and no souls to ferry, just worm food buried in dirt. There was irony here as it was Mr. Coachman who was the driver who ferried the bodies to Cooper before Cooper sent them to the underworld.

It was November, and everything was dying or dead. The trees had no leaves and the moon barely offered any light. Cooper was standing in a grave, digging in the late night fog. He was six feet tall, and the grave had been six feet deep; that is until after dark, and the hole had been made seven feet deep. Cooper threw his last shovelful of dirt out of the pit, then climbed out and sat there, with his feet dangling into the grave. He took a bottle of whiskey out of his coat pocket, opened it and had a drink, then lit a cigarette and began to smoke. He was waiting for Mr. Coachman.

Cooper did not wait long, for he was just finishing his cigarette when he was lit up by the headlights of Mr. Coachman's car. Cooper tossed the butt into the open grave and stood up, and when the engine cut out, he began walking towards the car. As he did, Mr. Coachman climbed out of the driver's door.

Their routine was always the same: Mr. Coachman would hand Cooper an envelope and Cooper would put it in his pocket, then they would walk to the back of Mr. Coachman's car, open the trunk and lift out a dead body wrapped in plastic. They would carry the body to the grave and toss it in the seven-foot hole. Next, Cooper would always jump back into the grave, dig two pennies out his pocket, un-wrap the corpse's face and place them over the dead man's eyes, then say: "Two pennies for the toll." After this, Cooper would tightly re-wrap the head so the pennies would remain where they had been placed; he did this so Charon, the ferryman, would find them.

Once Cooper was out of the grave, he pulled out a cigarette and began to light it with a match, and Mr. Coachman, who had been watching him lay pennies on the eyes of the dead for quite some time now, finally asked him, "What's that whole thing with the pennies all about?"

"Gotta pay the ferryman," Cooper replied as he tossed his match into the grave. He bent over, picked up the whiskey with one hand and the shovel with the other, then stood up and passed the bottle to Mr. Coachman and began to shovel a foot of dirt back into the grave, covering the body and leaving a six foot hole for the funeral that would follow in the morning.

Once the body was covered, Cooper took the whiskey back from Coachman and took a drink; Coachman looked around the graveyard.

"Coop," he said, "how many of these graves have we done this with now? Put an extra body in a hole the night before a funeral?"

"Thirteen," Cooper answered.

"And what do you think those thirteen families would say if they knew gramps had a roommate?"

"Fuck 'em, the holes were all deep enough," Cooper answered, and the two men laughed.

....

It was the day after the thirteenth body had been laid to rest. It was cold, grey, and as dead as November. There was a funeral, and a casket was being laid into a six-foot grave that had been seven foot deep just a few hours before...a grave that already contained a body.

From the caretaker's shack, the funeral was observed. The shack was several yards away, and standing there in front of the door was Cooper, a cigarette hanging from his mouth, the lit end creeping ever slowly away from the tip down towards the filter as the casket slowly descended into the ground to rest upon a corpse.

Once the casket was out of sight, Cooper put out his cigarette and smiled. He then reached into his pocket and produced the envelope Mr. Coachman had given him, an envelope filled with money. Cooper took his cut of bills, then closed it. The envelope went into his breast pocket, his bills into his pants pocket, and then he went into the shack.

The shack was as luxurious as the name suggests. It had shelves and racks that served as the homes for landscaping and digging tools, fertilizers, cleaning solutions and the like. There was an old wooden desk, and two old wooden chairs, and a space heater. Cooper turned it on to warm the space and then sat back in a chair, put his feet up on the desk, and waited for his boss to come pick up the envelope.

Cooper worked for a man named Mr. Necropolis, a figure as sinister and dark as the tombs found in his graveyard. Mr. Necropolis owned the cemetery, and he had no beliefs beyond cash-in-hand, no morality beyond what was relative to his own gains, and no patience for mistakes, which is why Cooper had never made one.

Cooper took out a cigarette and struck a match, then as he lit the nail, the door creaked open and Mr. Necropolis entered, followed by a younger man who nervously chewed on his thumbnail like an insecure child.

"You're not supposed to smoke in here, Coop," Necropolis said as he took the only other seat in the shed.

"I'm not supposed to do a lot of the things I do for you around here," Cooper replied, then he produced the envelope and passed it to Mr. Necropolis, who tucked it away in his pocket.

Mr. Necropolis turned and looked at the young man who had followed him into the shack with a cold November stare, and his smile died on his face.

"I hired you an assistant, Coop," Necropolis said with contempt and disdain bordering on hatred.

"Why?" Cooper asked. Cooper was a loner; he disliked people and he downright hated nervous people - they were always trouble.

"He's my wife's nephew, that's why. He went to prison twice and now no one will hire him, so she said I have to," Necropolis said, his contempt growing, evolving, with every word.

"What did he do wrong?" Cooper asked.

"He got caught," Necropolis replied with disappointment and agitation, and Cooper knew from his boss' tone that he would need to watch the new guy.

"Filcher, this is Cooper," Mr. Necropolis continued, addressing his nephew, "When he says dig, you dig. You work at night and always stay clear of funerals."

Necropolis rose and walked out, and Cooper began to examine Filcher with disdain. As the door to the shack creaked back to a close, Cooper could see the fear in Filcher's eyes, and he smiled.

"So what goes on here? What do we do?" Filcher asked, breaking the silence as he chewed on his thumbnail, showing his fear.

"It's a graveyard, we fucking dig, and no matter what, you see nothing, you hear nothing, you keep your mouth fucking shut about this place. To everyone," Cooper snarled.

"R-relax man," Filcher stuttered. "I was just breaking the ice."

"Don't!" Cooper barked in an icy snarl, as he leaned back in his chair and closed his eyes.

....

It was dark and misty in the graveyard on Filcher's first night there, and the moon was pale. He was fearful and skittish by nature; he was also superstitious … and claustrophobic. He was only five feet and five inches tall, made more conspicuous when he was standing in an open grave. The grave was already six feet deep before Cooper had ordered Filcher to climb in, putting the banks well above his head, and every time he looked up and tried to toss more dirt out, he believed he could see the banks growing higher, causing him to sink deeper into the grave; by the time it was seven feet deep, he was nearly in tears with hysteria.

Filcher was looking up, and he could not see Cooper at all, and this put him on the edge of a panic attack.

"C-Cooper, hey Cooper," Filcher began to call out, "are you there, man?!"

After several long moments, moments that were the briefest of seconds in the passage of time but a painful eternity for Filcher, he heard Cooper's smoky voice, but he could still not see him as he looked up. He could only see the banks of dirt stretching up forever towards the sky, closing in around him, forcing him down, shrinking him into an expanding darkness and entombing him among the dead.

"After your body dies," Cooper's voice said from out of

sight, "your soul will be trapped here unless you have enough money to pay the ferryman to take you across the river Styx."

Cooper's words chilled Filcher to the bone.

"C-come on, man," Filcher pleaded, "get me out of here! It must be deep enough now?"

And as the cold sweat ran down his brow, Filcher saw Cooper look down into the grave, a lit cigarette in his mouth. Cooper tossed the cigarette into it, then held out his hand. Filcher slapped the handle of the shovel into Cooper's palm and holding on to the other end, used it to climb out of the grave frantically. Cooper was laughing.

Once he was on the earth's surface, Filcher fell to the ground in a panic, tears running down his face. He could still hear Cooper laughing at him, but it felt like the laughter was miles away as he fought to regain control of his breathing. Eventually, Filcher had composed himself and sat up to look around. He saw that Cooper was sitting on a headstone and looking down the dirt road that ran throughout the graveyard while smoking a cigarette.

Although he was embarrassed by his pathetic spectacle, he worked up the confidence to swallow his pride, mostly due to the fear of being left alone in the graveyard, and he decided to join Cooper.

Filcher sat down beside him on the headstone and found the silence and dark were an unholy combination, so he spoke: "Hey man, can I bum one of those smokes?"

"Fuck off," Cooper replied.

"That's okay," Filcher said, as if Cooper cared, "I don't really smoke anyway."

As soon as Filcher was finished his last word it was too silent for him, so he continued to speak, and Cooper continued to ignore him.

"So, my uncle mentioned I went to prison," Filcher began, "First time I went up was for joyriding in a stolen car - did eighteen months." He waited only a beat, and once he realized Cooper was not going to reply, he continued: "The second time, though, that was for an armed robbery, and I did five years."

Finally, Filcher had said something interesting enough to elicit a reply from Cooper.

"You only got a nickel for an armed robbery?" a skeptical Cooper asked.

"Well, I wasn't armed with a gun, so I think that helped the sentencing," Filcher replied, becoming a little more comfortable now that there was another voice in the darkness.

"What did you have?" Cooper asked.

"A bat," Filcher said, proudly.

"A bat?" Cooper replied, confused.

"Yeah, man, a bat," Filcher boasted.

"You are fucking stupid."

"Well, the way I figured it, if I got caught with a gun, I could be looking at ten or fifteen years."

As Filcher was speaking, he heard the sounds of tires on the dirt road, and then suddenly he and Cooper were caught in the headlights of Mr. Coachman's car.

"Go away - now," Cooper ordered Filcher as he stood

up and tossed his cigarette butt.

"Who's that?"

"Ain't no one here but you and I," Cooper snarled.

"No, really man, who is this?" Filcher insisted.

"I told you, there ain't no one here. You see nothing, you hear nothing, and you keep your fucking mouth shut," Cooper barked.

"C'mon Cooper..." Filcher began.

"One more fucking word and I will bury you in that open grave," Cooper said. "Now go away!"

Filcher stood up, and scared to death of going back into that hole in the ground, began to walk away from Cooper without another word.

Filcher retreated into the darkness somewhat, and found a place to spy on Cooper; he could still see him as the headlight from the car lit the graveyard.

As he watched, Mr. Coachman climbed out of the car and handed Cooper an envelope. Next, the two men walked to the trunk and took something out. It was a large item, and to Filcher it appeared to be slumped, dead weight. He watched the two men carry it to the open grave Filcher had been standing in just moments earlier and saw them throw it in; with horror, Filcher realized it had to be a body.

Next, he saw Cooper jump into the grave for a brief moment, and then climb back out, grab the shovel, and begin to throw dirt into the hole. Filcher had seen enough to know something was wrong, so he retreated to the caretaker's shack and called his uncle.

. . . .

At the caretaker's shack, Filcher paced nervously, chewing on his thumbnail, growing more and more skittish with each passing minute, until finally he heard the door open and turned to see Mr. Necropolis.

"Am I glad to see you!" Filcher exclaimed.

"Filcher, I don't like graveyards," Necropolis answered with agitation in his tone. "I know, I know ... I own this cemetery, but to be honest these places creep me out, especially at night."

"I'm sorry, but trust me, this is important, man," Filcher pleaded, nervously.

"It had better be! I don't appreciate being made to come here more than I need to," Necropolis warned his nephew.

"I know, but it's Cooper," Filcher said, nervously.

"Cooper? You got me out here for a damned digger?! This better be worth my time, Filcher!"

Necropolis was now beyond angry, and Filcher could tell.

"You don't understand," Filcher pleaded, "he's putting something in the graves…it looked like a body."

"Bodies into a grave," Necropolis said with derision, "Well, there's an idea!"

He was staring hard at Filcher, and Filcher was beginning to grow uneasy when the door to the caretaker's shack creaked open.

"Well, speak of the devil and the devil will waltz on your

grave," Necropolis said as Cooper entered.

Cooper looked slowly from the older man to the younger, and then back to Necropolis.

"You never come out here at night," Cooper stated to his boss as he shoved past Filcher to his desk, opened the top drawer, and pulled out a bottle of whiskey.

"Filcher said he saw you drop something into an open grave earlier tonight," Necropolis said.

"Nope," Cooper answered the accusation, dryly and dishonestly.

"Well, there you go, Filcher. Thank you, Coop, everything is clear now," Necropolis said, laying the issue to rest. "You can go."

Cooper gave a nod to his boss, and retreated out of the shack methodically, closing the door behind him, sealing Filcher and Necropolis inside.

"Feel better?" Mr. Necropolis asked his nephew.

"No," Filcher pleaded. "He's fucked up, man. I'm telling you, something is going on here! What are we going to do?!"

"We? I'm going home, you are going to go do your damned job and dig a hole," Necropolis replied, losing what little patience he had left.

"What?!" Filcher asked, confused and scared. He was terrified about being alone in the graveyard with Cooper.

"Do you want him even angrier with you?!" Necropolis snapped.

"B-b-but..." Filcher stammered, "we have to do something. He's hiding bodies in the open graves."

"Trust me," Necropolis said in a soothing voice. "Go dig. I will sort this out." He put his hand on his nephew's shoulder and smiled. "I will take care of you," he said.

Noticeably calmer, Filcher made his return to work, leaving Mr. Necropolis alone in the shed, where his soothing expression grew darker.

. . . .

There had not been a funeral scheduled at the graveyard

for several days, and now November itself was dying off, transitioning into the dead months of winter; but before November was to be buried in time, another funeral was scheduled, and the night before, a six-foot grave needed to be deepened to seven.

It was snowing large fluffy flakes that night, the sort of snow that never amounts to much, but still can soak through your clothes and leave your bones chilled if you're exposed to it long enough. Filcher was in the grave, and every time loose dirt began to cascade in on him, he felt as though Cooper was beginning to bury him. He was scared; he had been waiting for his uncle to make good on his promise to handle Cooper, which he had taken to mean he would fire the caretaker as soon Filcher had learned the ropes; but digging was a simple task and Cooper was still there after more than two weeks.

When he had reached seven feet deep, Filcher called out to Cooper, who came over, grabbed the shovel handle and helped Filcher out of the grave. Cooper then sat on a nearby headstone and lit a cigarette. Filcher still did not like being alone at night in the graveyard, so he went to join Cooper, but this time he remained standing, leaning on the shovel, as if it would protect him. The two men remained deathly silent, until they heard the sounds of a car traveling along the dirt road. When the headlights illuminated them, Filcher spoke.

"I'll just get out of the way now, Cooper."

He began to turn, but Cooper stood up and grabbed him by the arm, and smiled.

"Naw, you should stick around," he said.

"Why?" Filcher had a very bad feeling.

"Trust me," Cooper replied, a sparkle showing in his usually dead eyes.

Filcher stood there, his eyes locked with Cooper's, feeling trapped, as if the entire graveyard was closing in around him. Then he heard the car doors open and close, two of them, and he turned his head to look at the car. At first he saw nothing except the headlights, but he could hear the crunchy footsteps of hard soles on snow and dirt, and then two men emerged into the light; one was Mr. Coachman, the man he had seen with Cooper before, and the other his uncle, Mr. Necropolis.

Filcher felt more at ease for a moment upon seeing his uncle, but then he noticed Cooper had stepped back away from him, and the three formed a semi-circle around him. On instinct, a nervous Filcher began to back up until he realized the heels of his shoes had reached the edge of the open grave. Filcher came to a stop, terrified.

"We gave it a name," Mr. Coachman said, with sinister pride in his voice, "that extra hole you dig under the graves. Coop, did you tell him what we call it?"

"No," Cooper replied.

"The dirt road," Mr. Coachman said smiling. "We tried dirt road to hell, but you know how these things are, you shorten names of things over time. Lazy speech I guess."

"I...I...I don't understand ...?" Filcher replied, confused.

"And that is exactly the problem," Necropolis joined in. "You're a fuck up. And I will not let you fuck this up for me." He grew angrier, more agitated, more determined. "You should have listened to Cooper, Filcher. You should have seen nothing, and you never should have called me."

Mr. Necropolis let out a sigh, and he nodded to Cooper; Cooper swiftly grabbed the shovel out of Filcher's hands, pulled it back, and sunk it into the young man's face, simultaneously killing him and knocking him into the open grave.

Cooper dropped the shovel and jumped into the hole. He looked into Filcher's face, searching for the eyes through its blood-filled, fractured remains. Once he felt the eye sockets, he fished through his pocket and pulled out two pennies. He placed one penny over each eye, pressing them into the blood so they would stick to the dead face.

He then whispered to the corpse,

"Two pennies for the toll."

Always

Connor was 43, and he was sitting in his doctor's office. Not in the waiting room, and not in the exam room, but in the office. Connor had been going to the same doctor for over twenty years, and this was the first time he had ever been in the actual office; in fact, until today he had no idea it existed. Of course it did exist, and it made sense to him that it did once he had been brought into it, but he had never thought about it before. And now that Connor was sitting in it, he had pretty well surmised what would come next.

Connor sat in the chair, stoically facing forward, looking past the desk and out the window, waiting. From behind him, Connor heard the door open and close as the doctor entered. He walked past Connor, carrying the patient's file flattened against his hip as he walked, and sat down on the edge of his desk. He set his physician's hand on Connor's shoulder in a kindly manner, but offered only a grave expression.

"Well doc," Connor said, breaking the clinical silence, "I wouldn't have wanted to overstay my welcome anyway."

After his meeting with his doctor, Connor went home and sat down in the kitchen of his small apartment, the bane of a single, middle-aged man who lost all his momentum in his thirties. He just sat and thought for a long time, reflecting. At that moment when one dies, it is said one's life flashes before one's eyes, but where Connor's death was slow in coming to him - somewhere in the ballpark of two to three months - his life did not flash before his eyes; instead, it sauntered. His life strolled out in front of him at a deliberate and methodical pace, and all the best moments, all the triumphs and rewards, all the tragedies that were overcome, all the best fun and all the greatest hopes, always led his thoughts back to Stephanie.

They had met at a low point in his life, and, because of her, that life transformed instantly. They went on to have many good years together, until something about Connor changed. Connor had known something was wrong, and he was beginning to have severe trouble with basic tasks and focus. His work suffered, his stress elevated, his home life deteriorated, and Connor knew he was sick. No one, however, believed him; not Stephanie, not his employer, not even his doctor. And so cast off in the role of fool, everything in Connor's life fell apart. The stress was too much for his relationship with Stephanie, and Connor found himself single and, soon thereafter, unemployed; now, just a few short years later, his doctor discovered Connor had been right all along.

As the flashbacks of his life drew to a close, Connor realized he only had one outstanding matter left he needed to tend to if he wanted to set his affairs in order, so he walked to the telephone, a land line mounted on his kitchen wall, and he dialed her number, and he left her a message.

A few hours later, Stephanie listened to Connor's message: "Hey ... It's - it's me. Been a long time. I know I'm not someone you want to hear from, but ... I need to see you, just for a few minutes. I need to settle my accounts. I'm dying. My routine hasn't changed. I still take my coffee in the same place, same time. I'll be doing it until ... well, you can find me there." It was a message that said all there was to say.

After he hung up the phone, Connor went to the junk drawer under his kitchen counter and pulled out a pen, a sheet of paper, and an envelope. He wrote something on the paper, folded it, then tucked it in the envelope, licked the back and sealed it. Across the front of the envelope he wrote her name, *Stephanie*. Connor did this just in case he ran out of time, and then, the way most people glance up at their kitchen clock, Connor glanced at the wall calendar in his kitchen. It was September.

The next morning, Connor got up and went through his morning routine. He showered, he shaved, he had a sensible breakfast, then he went for his walk, an hour out to the riverside park by foot. As he neared the park, Connor passed a coffee shop; he went in and purchased two cups of coffee and placed them in a cardboard tray, and then continued to the park and selected the same bench he selected every day, one that looked out at the river, and he sat down. Connor placed the tray beside him, reached into his pocket and removed the envelope with Stephanie's name on it, placed it in the cardboard tray, and leaned it up against one of the coffee cups. He picked up the other cup, tore open the tab on the lid, and began to drink the warm, black liquid in the crisp, cool air. When he was done his coffee, Connor put the envelope back in his pocket, stood up, and began the hour-long trek home.

As September transitioned into October, Connor continued to follow this exact routine, but once October had rolled in, he realized it was beginning to take him a little longer to reach the park, and when he arrived there he sat longer before returning home, but just the same he followed his routine. Connor walked to the park, picked up two coffees, sat on the same bench, leaned the same envelope against one coffee cup as he drank from the other, then picked up the envelope when he finished, and walked home.

By the time November arrived, Connor's morning routine stretched late into the afternoon, and the light was beginning to fade before he began his trek home; he was slowing down, but he had not missed a day.

Every day, the routine remained the same: Connor trekked to the park, sat on the bench, leaned the envelope against one coffee and drank the other. The only real change was how long he now sat on the bench, how long he rested, how long he recovered, and how long it took to prepare for his hard trek home.

November was drawing to a close and the weather had become cold, so Connor had to bundle up more, but he still trekked to the park every day, sat on the bench, and displayed Stephanie's letter in the same-like fashion as he drank his coffee.

Connor's routine had not changed at all until the final day of November; indeed, this day was different. Stephanie pulled into the parking lot at the park where Connor took his coffee. This had always been his routine and she knew he would be there, that he would go to the same bench he always did, so she took a deep breath, climbed out of her car and began to walk through the park to Connor's favorite spot.

As Stephanie walked along the path, she saw the river first, and then she saw the very bench Connor always sat on. Connor was there, his back to her, and so she paused to steady her nerves, and then after a few deep breaths, she resumed her march towards him.

As she approached, Stephanie noticed Connor seemed very still in the cold. She circled round the bench and stood in front of him to say hello. She took a breath and forced a smile to greet him, and only then realized Connor was slumped forward, peacefully in repose with his coffee spilled all over his shoes.

As Stephanie's smile faded with the realization of the scene in front of her, she noticed the cardboard tray with a second cup of coffee and an envelope with her name written across its front propped up against it. She picked up the envelope and opened it, and then pulled out the single piece of paper inside. She unfolded it and read what was written on it, and then Stephanie began to cry.

Connor's note to Stephanie was short and simply read:

Dear Stephanie,

ALWAYS,

- Connor

Ironically, Paris

The security guard found the man sitting at the bar at his departure terminal, waiting to board an international flight to Montreal, Canada. The man had been drinking in the terminal for more than a couple of hours, having had several hours to kill between the hotel check-out time and the departure time for his flight, free time during his last day in Paris he had chosen to spend there, at the airport.

The man had been at the airport for quite some time before his desired terminal had been ready for travelers, but like most large international airports, the *Charles de Gaulle* had many bars scattered about, so his first drinks had been on a different stool at a different bar in the same airport. As he drank, he fumbled about with a small box, small enough to fit in the palm of his hand.

There was nothing unique about the box itself other than it was from Paris. The box was a small, square, cheap cardboard thing, like many other boxes from many other places in many other cities.

The man was midway through his third whiskey when he had heard the announcement that his flight had been assigned a terminal and was now open, so when he reached the bottom of his glass, the man placed the small box in his pocket and began to migrate towards his terminal to await his boarding call. As he walked, he had thought he heard his name paged by airport security, but since he did not know anyone in Paris, he just shook it off as a trick of his ears, like he had experienced many times before, and he continued to walk to his terminal.

Once the man had found his terminal, he found the bar. He selected a stool identical to the one at the first bar, which was in all ways identical to this second bar, and he ordered a drink identical to those he had been drinking at the first bar.

He took out his small, simple cardboard box and began to play with it like he had played with it before.

The man was halfway through his third drink at this second bar in the same airport when again he thought he heard his name paged by airport security. Once again, he simply shook off the page as coincidence, surmising someone else travelling through Paris had a name identical to his own. It was not until he reached the bottom of his glass that he realized the page had indeed been for him.

A security guard tapped him on the shoulder, and when the man turned, he saw the security guard shaking his head back and forth slowly, with a stern expression on his face and a passport in his hand.

"Yours, *monsieur*," the security guard stated, passing the document to the man.

"Thank you," the man replied; he set the small box down on the bar and accepted his passport from the guard.

"*Monsieur*," the guard said, "you will need it to board the plane."

The guard laughed politely at his own friendly remark, identical to many friendly remarks of jest made in airports all over the world.

"Yes, I suppose I will," the man replied. "*Merci*."

The guard slid onto the stool next to the man and smiled amicably.

"*Pardonne-moi, monsieur*, may I ask how you could lose your passport in the airport? A trans-Atlantic flight is very expensive, and had we not found it, you would have no way to get on a new flight, even if you did buy a new plane ticket."

"Well, my friend, I guess I just need supervision," he answered flatly, and this made the guard smile.

"Then perhaps, *monsieur*, what you really need is a wife," the guard suggested as a joke.

"That's actually why I came to Paris," the man replied.

"Ahh, I see," the guard said. "Paris is well known for *amour*, and there are many wonderful Parisian women, but to meet and marry one while on a holiday may not have been realistic." The guard still believed they were joking.

"I had a better plan than that," the man replied.

"Oh," the guard queried, raising an inquisitive eyebrow, now realizing they had not been joking.

"I came to Paris to propose."

The man looked down at his empty glass and waved to the bartender, who poured him a new whiskey and accepted a bill as payment; all the while, the guard remained silent, waiting for the man to continue.

"I thought Paris would be the most romantic place to make the grandest of romantic gestures."

"Indeed, *monsieur*, it is true for most," the guard said. "May I ask what went wrong? Did she say no?"

"She never showed up," the man said, then laughed sadly.

"*Monsieur...?*" the guard asked, confused.

"I had sent her travel plans, a plane ticket … and I came here to wait," the man explained. "It was a surprise, it was … romantic."

"But why?" the guard asked. "Why would you just not include her in the planning? It was a great risk, *monsieur.*"

"Paris requires a grand romantic gesture, and she …" the man trailed off for a moment, "… she deserved one."

The man and the guard sat for a few moments in silence at the bar in the terminal at the *Charles de Gaulle* airport, and then they heard the announcement calling for all passengers traveling to Montreal to board the plane. After the announcement had been made, they sat a little longer until the page for final call to board was made.

"*Monsieur,*" the guard said to the man, bringing him back in to reality. "That is last call for your flight."

The man came back to his senses. He turned his eyes towards the gate, and he saw the last boarding passenger showing his passport to the airline representative and heading towards the plane. The man looked down at his last whiskey in Paris sitting on the counter. He picked it up and raised his glass to the guard and toasted: "Ironically, Paris." Then he shot the entire glass back stiffly, stood up, and began to walk to the gate, passport in hand.

"*Monsieur*," the guard called after him, "is this not yours as well?"

The man turned around as the guard picked up the man's box and held it high to show it to him.

"That is nothing," the man said. "Just a souvenir that would have only followed me home and found its way into a drawer and been lost inside that drawer forever. You keep it. A *petite cadeau* to thank you for finding my passport."

Bidding the guard "*Au revoire*", he turned and walked the remaining distance to the gate.

"*Au revoire, mon ami*," the guard called after him. "*Et merci!*"

After the man had boarded the plane, the way travelers do in airports all over the world, the guard stood up and walked to the window where he could watch the airplane taxi its way to the tarmac, the way people do to watch planes take flight in airports. He watched the airplane travel down the runway, away from *Charles de Gaulle* airport, and climb into the sky, travelling away from Paris, France, as departing flights always do when they leave Paris behind, and then, with his new friend well on his way, the guard turned his attention to the small box, the gift the man had left him.

The guard opened the box and in it he found a diamond ring.

Rourke

Detective Rourke was halfway through his third glass of gin when the bartender's attention was called away from his newspaper by the sound of the telephone. Rourke sighed deeply, knowing what news the telephone would bring. He did not carry a cell phone, but it was not difficult to find him, and his instincts told him that was exactly why the phone in the bar was ringing.

Rourke was a fifty-year-old homicide cop with a taste for gin and general dislike of everything else. He was disheveled, unkempt, and defeated, and he had been this way for several years. His career was terminal, not because he was a poor detective; in fact, his deductive skills were astounding, but nonetheless his career progress stopped, and he watched as many less deserving and less experienced police officers were promoted up the ranks ahead of him, most of whom could not catch a hooker in a whorehouse. Rourke was very good, but he was never anyone's favorite personality. Of course, that alone was not what had led to his accelerated deterioration.

When Rourke was in his late thirties, he should have been on the verge of a promotion; he had closed more cases than anyone in his precinct's history and he had gone to night school to earn his degree. Being a good detective, he came to realize none of that would matter - he was never getting the nod, he was not political nor polished, and as he was not suited for any other profession, he was locked in, *terminal.* The job that Rourke had once enjoyed had become a prison, and being a natural-born cynic, those hard feelings followed him home night after night, until one night he arrived home to a hollow sounding lock, greeted only by the echoes of his footfalls as he moved through the deserted house. That was his fortieth birthday, ten years ago.

The bartender answered the ringing phone, then passed it on to the detective, who put the receiver to his ear.

"Yeah?" Then after a moment, Rourke asked, "Where is that?"

Without adding anymore, the detective gave the phone receiver back to the bartender and then proceeded to finish his gin. He stood up, dropped a bill on the bar, and walked out.

The crime scene was a small home in a small subdivision on the outskirts of town on a treed-in quarter acre lot, creating an allusion of seclusion. The scene was typical: a couple of squad cars were out in front of the house with their lights flashing, sirens off, a few patrolmen moving about and going through the motions while others just stood around; it was like any workplace really. Rourke parked his car, reached into the glove box, took out his badge and gun, and slid them both into his coat pocket; he then climbed out of his car and began to walk to the house.

As he approached the front door, Rourke dug out his badge and held it out to show the patrolman on sentry duty, who, in turn, nodded to the detective as he passed.

Upon entering the front room, Rourke noted how small the home really was; in fact, it was smaller on the inside than it appeared on the outside. There were only three rooms: the main room, which was a living area with a kitchenette set into it on one side; a bedroom; and a bathroom. Both the bedroom and bathroom doors were open, and there was a patrolman and second detective in the main section waiting for Rourke to arrive.

Detective Sykes was standing by the bedroom door, a little pale and clammy looking; this told Rourke the body was inside the bedroom, and it was the first corpse Sykes had ever seen, at least in a professional capacity before the undertaker had a chance to work.

Sykes looked up as Rourke entered. He watched as the older detective took in the surroundings, turning his head about, studying every inch of the home, as if he had never been in a house before. After a moment, Sykes called out to him: "You must be Rourke?"

"Yea, sorry 'bout your luck," Rourke replied dismissively.

"My name is Sykes. I'm new to homicide. This is my first case. The captain told me he was assigning me as your partner."

Sykes was excited. It was his first day and he had dreamt of being a detective since he was a young boy; he still had the ambition and naiveté of a young man on the precipice of a grand adventure. By contrast, Rourke was gruff, bitter and always annoyed; he had already determined there was no need for him to be there, with neither a great mystery to solve, nor any master criminals to apprehend.

"Coroner been here yet?" Rourke asked.

"No, sir," Sykes answered

"Forensic team?"

"On the way."

"When they get here, tell them it was suicide. Have the coroner send the report downtown. When we get it, we'll file it together."

Rourke began walking to the front door.

"Detective," Sykes called after him, "don't you want to see the body? Or wait for the coroner or forensics team?"

"No, I don't need to. I already solved the case," Rourke said.

"How? You haven't even examined the actual crime scene?"

"No, but I read the suicide note," Rourke replied. "Stay, watch the forensics guys, learn what they do. And welcome to homicide, Detective Sykes."

Rourke turned his back to the crime scene and exited through the front door.

Detective Sykes was a little underwhelmed by his first meeting with the veteran detective. He had been told that Rourke was a bit stand-offish, but more importantly that he was a brilliant detective, so despite his first impression of

Rourke, Sykes was very much looking forward to working with the senior detective and learning from him, mastering the techniques of observation and deduction.

Reflecting on Rourke's arrival and departure, Sykes began to wonder if the senior detective had actually just shown him how to use observation and deduction to come to a conclusion. Sykes walked to the point in the room where Rourke had stood, and like Rourke, he began to look around the room as if it was the first time he had ever been in one.

Sykes deconstructed the room based on what makes a room a room, what elements were present in any room. He thought of walls, ceilings, floors, doorways, doorknobs, and even furnishings, and he could say without a doubt that this room had all of those components, but then the *state* of the furnishings struck him.

They were suitable for one, a single person, period. There was not enough furniture for a second person, even if that second person was simply a visitor. There was one lamp in the main room, and one chair. The kitchenette had a single stool at the breakfast counter, and when Sykes opened the cupboard he found only one plate, one bowl, one glass, and one coffee mug. He looked around the room and realized there were no paintings or photographs, no sculptures, calendars, or any markings for that matter. There were no shelves, there were no books; the room had all the components necessary to make it a room, but the house had none of the components necessary to make it a home.

Sykes began to wonder if this was the same conclusion that Rourke had reached, and he began to think he had learned something from the senior detective after all.

The crime scene was at the front of Sykes' mind when he arrived at the police station the next morning. He was looking forward to sharing his thoughts on the case with his new partner, but as the morning crept on, Detective Rourke failed to report in for duty. Sykes had asked the captain about this, and he was told it was not unusual for Rourke to be late, sometimes more than half a day late, and that usually it was due to his being hung-over and had he not been such a brilliant detective, they would never put it up with it. As the day dragged on, Rourke failed to appear; by the afternoon, Sykes decided something was wrong.

He dug up Rourke's address and made his way over to the senior detective's house. As he approached the home, Sykes noticed nothing unusual. It was a small duplex, and Rourke's car was in the driveway. Sykes pulled his vehicle in and parked it behind Rourke's, then climbed out and went to the front door.

His knock received no answer, so he knocked a second time only to achieve the same result. He tried the door and discovered it was unlocked. Pushing the door open, he stepped into the foyer and called out for his partner, but was met with silence.

Sykes stepped through the foyer into the living room and he stopped dead in his tracks. On an old chesterfield, worn and weathered in need of upholstery repair, Rourke was slumped over. At the older man's feet was an empty bottle of gin.

Sykes remained still; he turned his attention to Rourke's living room. The remote control was on top of the television and under easily four inches of dust; clearly it had not been turned on in years. Other than the worn chesterfield, there was a small well-stained coffee table, and no other furniture. The walls were bare, with a hint of wear in spots to indicate that at one time, long ago, there had been items hung on there, presumably photographs, but now, nothing. There was no radio anywhere to be seen, and no indication that any real life had taken place in the home in many years.

Rourke's home was his note.

Roll On Three

Tears stained the metal plate. They began to flow freely once Louie the Fourteenth had swallowed his last bite and realized with horror it was over; his life was over. It was ending, and he could not change that. For the first time in fourteen months, Louie finally experienced the paradigm shift in his thinking that allowed him to internalize and process the reality of his fate. Louie Chill, a.k.a. Louie the Fourteenth, had eaten his last meal, and in only a few hours the great state of Texas would see him out of this world.

Louie the Fourteenth had been sentenced to death row at the James H. Byrd Unit in Huntsville, Texas, in the early part of 1948; and after his appeals had failed, the judge had sentenced Louie to die on October 14th, 1951. Whether or not the sentencing judge had a dark sense of humor, or if it was just a coincidence that Louie the Fourteenth was to die on the 14th day of the month, had been a subject of debate and speculation among the guards and inmates alike.

For his last meal, Louie had enjoyed a steak prepared rare, with a baked potato, an ear of corn, and a root beer; for dessert, he had a slice of devil's food cake and a large glass of milk. It had been important that Louie's meal be properly prepared and thoroughly satisfying as it was his last, and this gesture was the very least society could offer a man before executing him. This is not to say Louie was a good man; he was not, but killing was killing and executions are philosophically no different from murders. They were cold, pre-meditated, and preyed on the defenseless, and it was this sense of defenselessness and finality that had reduced Louie to hysterical tears. Louie was going to die, and he could do nothing about it.

Louie was now living the state of terror that always precedes a violent death, the same terror that his victims had experienced before *their* deaths, and the same terror that any man fearful of death would experience while approaching the hour of his execution. Louie did not handle it stoically.

Louie's sobs drifted out of his cell and travelled along the cold corridor of death row. The guards heard him and dismissed Louie's sobs; they had heard this before from many others. The other inmates heard him as well, and some were filled with terror knowing it would someday be them; others just ignored him, blocking out the sounds of Louie's tears. One inmate, Amos Miller, was different ... he was cruel.

Perhaps Miller was in denial that he would share the same fate as Louie, or perhaps he was just rotten on the inside, but Miller hurled insults and taunted Louie, and the more Louie cried, the more Miller mocked him.

Paddy Ryan was the opposite kind of inmate of Amos Miller. Ryan was very aware that his own death was coming too, but he tried to remain stoic despite his empathy for

Louie.

To Ryan, Louie's crying was a reminder that there was no dignity in how these men had lived their lives, nor was there much room for it in how they were to die. Ryan knew that facing certain death would be enough to take the mettle out of most men. It was neither probable nor theoretical death, and there wasn't any chance to avoid it. There was only one opportunity to usher the other inmates out with compassion, and that compassion was found only in the simple inaction of not tormenting them. Ryan also knew many more men would cry as they met their fates at James H. Byrd Unit in Huntsville, Texas, and secretly he prayed that by some miracle he would not be one of them.

As time crept on slowly, Louie would cry harder and harder, and then he would stop for a little while; after a short time, he would begin to sob again, and the sobs would grow louder, and he would cry harder, again and again. This pattern repeated until the priest arrived to offer Louie the last rites.

Louie was sobbing when prison boss Reilly stepped to his cell door with Father Mulligan. Louie didn't hear them approach, and they waited until he noticed them. After a few moments, Louie looked up and saw the priest standing beside Boss Reilly, and he became silent and hopeful.

"Louie," Boss Reilly said, "Father Mulligan has come to offer you the last rites."

"And to hear your confession, if you wish," Father Mulligan added.

"Yes," Louie said emphatically, "yes, please Father, please! I want the sacraments of confession and the last rites. Please."

Louie's voice was cracking, and it was composed of a mixture of hope and fear. Father Mulligan had heard voices like this before, in situations just like this one. The priest had offered the Last Rites and taken confessions from Catholics, Baptists, Jews, Buddhists, atheists, and even satanists during their last hours at James H. Byrd Unit. Some of them were Christians motivated by a general feeling of remorse; some of them were not Christians but were searching for a dignified end or moment of catharsis; and still others were non-repentant but confessing out of a fear of the impending abyss that would take them.

Father Mulligan nodded to Boss Reilly, who unlocked the prison cell door and slid it open. The priest stepped inside Louie's cell, and Boss Reilly closed and locked the door before he walked away, his footsteps echoing into the silence, leaving Louie and Father Mulligan in as much privacy as was allowed.

Alone, or as alone as death row permitted, Louie the fourteenth first confessed to Father Mulligan that was he not sure if he had ever even been baptized into any religion; he had no recollection of ever having been in a church before. Nevertheless, Father Mulligan went on to hear his confession and offer him the last rites just the same, and Louie did calm somewhat, taking moderate comfort with what the priest was doing for him.

As Louie's visit with Father Mulligan drew to an end,

Boss Reilly returned to Louie's cell door along with two prison guards, and spoke to the condemned man:

"It's time, Louie," Boss Reilly said simply, and then Louie fell to his knees as the prison boss nodded to a guard, who put a key into the cell door, unlocked it, and slid it open.

The instant that revolved around unlocking Louie's door seemed to last forever. The sound of the key, metal on metal, sliding into the keyhole moved slowly through Louie's ears, and the *click, click, click* of the lock mechanism moving over metal teeth and releasing, grew louder and louder with each release, making the sliding sound of the prison cell door opening the most frightening thing that Louie had ever heard, and he would have given anything to be allowed to remain inside that tiny, cold cell.

Once the door was opened wide, Louie looked long at Boss Reilly, and he fought hard not to start to cry again.

"Be calm, my son," Father Mulligan spoke softly.

"Do you think, Father," Louie asked with a trembling voice, "that I am too late to save?"

"My son," Father Mulligan answered, "it is not my place to presume the will of God. All I can do is offer guidance and comfort."

Louie listened carefully to Father Mulligan, then the priest noticed the criminal's lips began to tremble.

"Are you familiar with the story of Jesus and the two thieves?" Father Mulligan asked.

"No, no I am not," Louie said in earnest, searching for words of comfort.

"Father," Boss Reilly interrupted, "we do need to go."

"Mr. Reilly," Father Mulligan offered, "this will only take a moment and I do think it will help."

The priest looked at Boss Reilly, who paused and thought only for a moment before nodding his approval. Father Mulligan smiled thinly in thanks, and then turned his attention back to Louie.

"When Jesus was Crucified, he was not alone. There were two other crucifixions that day, two criminals, one on his left, and one on his right. As they hung on their crosses, one of them mocked Jesus, showed no remorse for what he had done, and revealed himself a cruel man. The other one, however, was different; he defended Jesus to the first criminal, pointing out that they, the two thieves, were being punished justly whereas Jesus had done nothing wrong."

Father Mulligan paused for a moment to study Louie's face; the sentenced man was listening with earnest intensity.

"The second criminal then asked Jesus to remember him."

"And ... ?" Louie asked the priest. "And ... what happened?"

"Jesus replied to the criminal by saying, *'Truly I say to you today, you shall be with Me in Paradise.'*"

Father Mulligan looked at Louie, whose face was somewhat hopeful, and yet somewhat confused. Boss Reilly and the guards, too, all looked confused, unsure of the point the priest was trying to make.

"What this means, my son," Father Mulligan continued, "is only you and the Lord can know what is in your heart; if you are truly penitent, you can be saved. If your remorse is genuine, then your penance may well be paid. You, more than I, are in a position to know where your heart is… where your faith is."

And then Father Mulligan nodded to Boss Reilly, who sent his men into the cell to put prison restraints on Louie; next, Louie was escorted out of the cell and on to the mile.

Boss Reilly led the way with a shackled Louie behind him, a guard on either side of him, and Father Mulligan bringing up the rear. This should have been a smooth and simple walk, and would have been if not for Amos Miller. As they passed Miller's cell, the cruel man chose to taunt Louie, taking delight in the clear fear Louie was dealing with as the condemned man marched to his gruesome fate.

"You are going to hell Louie, you hear me? *Hell!*" Miller called out. "They are going to put you in the chair, strap you tight and turn you to crispy chicken!"

Louie stutter-stepped and felt the weight of Miller's taunts, but then a voice from the cell adjacent to Miller's called out. The voice belonged to Paddy Ryan.

"Stay strong, Louie. I'll say a prayer for you," Ryan called out, and Louie seemed to walk a little straighter as they led him off down the mile.

From their cells, Ryan and Miller could hear the echoes of sterile footsteps fade into the cold prison, and the sounds of metal doors opening and closing to allow Louie and his escorts to pass through and march towards fate. Once they were well on their way, Ryan addressed Miller: "Why did you do that to him?"

"Cuz he's a piece of shit, man, a real piece of fucking shit," Miller replied.

"Like we ain't?" Ryan asked rhetorically, then he sat down on the cold prison floor of his cell, his back slumped against the wall that separated him from Miller, with his head bowed forward.

As Ryan sat quietly, Miller paced like a caged animal, back and forth in his cell. There was not much room for pacing, but the slapping sound of his footsteps was consistent, like a metronome, and Ryan lost himself in the consistency of the pattern. After nearly forty-five minutes, Miller stopped pacing and the silence that was re-introduced onto death row was deafening.

"Hey, Ryan!" Miller called out.

"Yea?" Ryan answered him, never moving, remaining in his slumped, sitting posture against the wall.

"I was making the time since they took Louie, pacing."

"So?" Ryan replied with little interest.

"So… right about now the boss is saying '*roll on one*', and the first switch is being pulled."

"Un-huh," Ryan replied.

"They need to pull three switches in sequence, one then the other, and then the last one is the one that fries him, the others build a charge - you know that?" Miller asked, excited.

Ryan ignored him for a few moments, but then Miller changed the topic.

"You ain't really going to say a prayer for him, are you?"

"Yes, I am," Ryan said, unmoving, with his head still

bowed.

"Why?!" Miller snapped. "Why would you do that? Why would you do that for him?"

"Because maybe then someone will say a prayer for me when it's my time to sit in that chair," Ryan answered.

"Shit, man," Miller replied with great agitation, "do you really think it makes a difference?"

"I hope so," Ryan stated solemnly.

"So, you into God and all that?" Miller sneered.

"Yes," Ryan answered.

"Well that sort of makes you a hypocrite, doesn't it?" Miller said, "considering your life and all the sin."

"Yeah, a hypocrite and a lot worse," Ryan admitted.

"Well shit, man, it don't matter. Ain't no heaven, and if there were, none of us is going there, especially not Louie the Fourteenth."

"Well, not with that attitude," Ryan mocked. "But I believe in redemption."

"Naw man, there ain't no redemption – none," Miller

said, "and if there were, there ain't going to be none for Louie. He's a bad man."

"We're all in the same cage," Ryan replied.

"Yea, right," Miller said, dismissingly. "Do you even know why they call him Louie the Fourteenth?"

"No," Ryan admitted.

"Because he is a sick motherfucker, man, a stone cold killer ... just *sick*. No way he's redeemable," Miller replied, nearly giddy talking about Louie now.

"Aren't you in here for burning people alive?"

"No way - I burned them until they were dead," Miller said with glee.

"And *Louie* is sick ..." Ryan replied sarcastically.

"Yea. Ok," Miller continued, "check it out: they called him Louie the Fourteenth because he killed 14 young girls, all of them 14 years old, each one on the 14th day of the month, for 14 straight months."

"Yeah, sick," Ryan dryly replied, "but did he burn them?"

"Hey," Miller objected, "that was how I made my money, it was just business. Besides, you're a cop killer." Miller took a moment to pace and compose himself, and then continued. "Besides, I was earning a living. Louie just did it for kicks, man."

Both men became silent for a few minutes, and then Miller spoke again, breaking the silence.

"Right about now, the boss is calling out for them to '*roll on two*'."

Ryan raised his head, then he stood up, stretched, and stepped to the front of his cell, where the bars separated him from the freedom of the corridor. Ryan was gazing beyond through the prison walls and looking at wide-open spaces in his mind's eye when Miller snapped him back to Huntsville.

"Smelled good, didn't it?"

"What did?" Ryan asked.

"Louie's steak," Miller said. "His last meal. It was mouth-watering, man."

"Funny, ain't it?" Ryan meditated, leaning further into

the bars of his cell.

"What is?" Miller asked, stepping to the bars of his own cell and leaning into them, trying to see Ryan as they spoke to each other.

"The whole last meal of a condemned man," Ryan replied. "They give us a last meal in here and everyone goes ape, like it somehow means something. Like it's dignified."

"Oh, fuck that," Miller said, a bit annoyed, "fuck that, man. If they are going to kill us, the least they can do is give us a decent dinner."

"Did you do that?" Ryan suddenly fired back.

"Do what?"

"Before you burned them people…"

"No. But I didn't lock them up in no cage first either," Miller said defensively.

"Oh, ok then," Ryan said, dismissively.

They sat in silence briefly for less than a moment before Miller re-started the conversation.

"So what are you going to have? You know, for your

last meal?"

"Nothing."

"Well shit, man, why not?" Miller probed.

"When you die, your bowels release," Ryan answered.

"So what, man?" Miller pushed. "It ain't like you gotta clean it up."

"I didn't live my life with much dignity," Ryan said. "I figure the least I can do is try to die with some."

"Not me, brother," Miller laughed. "I'm going to stuff myself like the g'damned Christmas turkey. I'm going out with absolutely no dignity and a lot of stink!" Miller chuckled a little and then added, "I still got three years to go though, before I can leave my legacy in that chair."

"That so?" Ryan asked nonchalantly.

"Yeah. What about you?"

"August."

"This August coming?"

"This August coming."

"Just six months to go brother," Miller chimed.

"Want to know the real irony?" Ryan teased.

"Sure man," Miller said eagerly.

"It's my birthday."

After Ryan announced the day of his execution was the same as the day of his birth, for a hiccup both men were silent, and then almost at the same instant, they laughed at the morbid irony of death finding a man on the day of his birth.

"Well shit, man, then you have to have a last meal if it's your birthday. At least have some birthday cake, man," Miller chuckled.

"You know what?" Ryan replied. "If I can get them to bring a slice of cake in for everyone on the mile, we'll all have cake with my death."

Both the condemned men once again began to share a laugh, and as they did, the lights on death row dimmed momentarily and the laughter stopped.

"Looks like they rolled on three," Ryan said solemnly.

A Friendly Conversation

They were large, fluffy flakes of snow, and they fluttered down from the sky above, blanketing the streets, benches, sidewalks, trees, and hedges and making them all look fresh and clean, like crisp linen. The weather was fairly mild, and as he approached the tavern, Murphy's breath crystallized in the air in front of him and hung there for a fraction of a moment before dissipating and being replaced by a new contrail of air from his lungs.

As Murphy approached the tavern door, he stopped and inhaled deeply and then exhaled. He thought about how much he enjoyed the invigorating sensation; the air was much sweeter here then it ever was back in *the Yard*.

Lungs filled with new fresh air, Murphy turned and squared himself to the tavern door, on which was adorned a wreath. This would be Murphy's first Christmas on the outside in quite some time, and although he would be spending his time alone watching television specials and eating spaghetti from a can, he was very thankful to be on the outside for the holidays. Murphy opened the door and stepped into the tavern.

Outside, the afternoon sun was reflecting off the pure, white snow and it was bright. Inside the tavern, it was very dark, and as he stood there in the midst of the stark contrast of the bright light behind him and the dark shadow in front of him, anyone already in the tavern would be able to see Murphy before he could see any of them. The air outside was fresh and free, but the air in the tavern was dirty... and stale with regret.

Murphy shook the snow off his overcoat, then removed it and hung it over his forearm; he did this to give himself a moment for his eyes to adjust to the darkness as he looked around the room. There were sad Christmas decorations hanging from the bar and around the windows, pitiful, old, dirty, and in need of repair. In one corner, there was an artificial tree that was losing pine needles, evidenced by the plastic pins gathered at the base of the tree. The tavern was a dive at best; it was just the sort of place to find criminals, and that is exactly whom he was there to meet.

Murphy scanned the room and did a head count. The first man he noted was the bartender, an intimidating sort with a teardrop tattoo under his left eye and more ink all around his knuckles, faded and bleeding together from poor tattooing, making the nub art unintelligible.

At the far end of the bar there was an old looking man reading a newspaper with a full mug of beer in front of him. In the back of the bar, an old pool table was in use by two dirty looking men. In the centre of the room was a collection of tables, only one of which had a customer, and it was that customer who was the man Murphy was looking for, and his name was Felix.

Felix was sitting at the table with a large mug of beer, complete with a slippery smile. He was a slight man, thin, wiry, and, from a distance, he appeared older than he actually was, a result of years of drug use and alcohol abuse. Felix's back was to the door.

Murphy was there to meet with Felix because Felix had tracked him down; of course, he knew Felix would as soon as he had been let out, so Murphy simply waited ... until one day his phone rang and it was Felix's voice on the other end.

Murphy walked to the table, pulled out one of the wooden chairs and tossed his overcoat over another chair, looking down at Felix silently; when Felix realized Murphy was standing there, he looked up.

"Murph!" Felix exclaimed with forced joy. "As soon as I heard you were out, I had to see you. I want to buy you a drink."

Felix gestured his hand to the chair and motioned for Murphy to sit down. Murphy did.

"So what would you like to drink?" Felix asked, waving the bartender over. Because he had a chronic post-nasal drip, Felix had the annoying habit of constantly sniffling.

"I got sober on the inside," Murphy said flatly.

"Naw. C'mon man, you were really a machine before. A beer? A whiskey? Have a drink," Felix urged.

"Even if I did still drink, it would be a violation of my parole, and somehow I just don't trust you not to dime me out and send me back."

The bartender with the teardrop tattoo arrived at the table.

"Now that hurts ... that hurts a lot," Felix said in what he believed to be a convincing tone. He turned to the bartender. "Get my friend here a drink and put it on my tab - anything he wants."

The bartender looked down at Murphy.

"Coffee. Black," Murphy said.

The bartender walked away without saying a word.

"Coffee?" Felix asked. "Really, man?"

Felix was impulsive and incapable of change, and he believed the same to be true of everyone. Big changes, small changes - they did not exist for Felix.

"Like I said," Murphy explained, "I got straight on the inside."

The bartender returned with Murphy's coffee and put it down in front of him. Murphy and the bartender exchanged a look that Felix failed to notice, one that would have suggested to anyone else in the room a level of familiarity between the two, indicating that this was not their first meeting.

"What's this all about, Felix?" Murphy asked as he sipped his coffee.

"Wow, calm down, man. No need to rush to the point," Felix answered him. "Let's relax, take our time, catch-up on the old days."

"I left the old days in the past. And I was content to leave you there too, so what do you want?"

"Ok. It's a job," Felix said as his tone changed, a register lower, more confidential, a little softer, a little more serious. "Big score this time too, *really* big."

"A job? With you?"

"Yeah, with me. We were a great team."

"What makes you think I would ever do another job with you?"

"Because, like I said, we were a great team," Felix smiled and took a drink of his beer.

From the back of the room, from the pool table, the sound of the cue ball colliding with the racked balls carried; the breaking of the balls, the beginning of a new game. Murphy leaned back in his chair.

"Where's my money, Felix?" Murphy suddenly asked.

"Well, c'mon, Murph, that was over five years ago," Felix answered in what he thought was a good rendition of a good-natured tone.

"Eight," Murphy corrected him. "Where is my fucking money, Felix?"

"Murph, it ain't like that," Felix pleaded.

"No? Then how is it?"

"Murph, it was the price of doing business. You know how it is."

"I kept my mouth shut, Felix; now, I want my money. I kept my mouth shut and you and George went free. Now pay me my money down for doing my damned part."

"George is dead, Murph," Felix offered as a distraction.

"I damned well know George is dead!" Murphy screamed. After a pause in which he composed himself, Murphy continued more calmly. "I know George is dead, and I know he would not have spent, or divided the money out, until after I was a free man. George was a gentlemen's thief, not that there are any of them left now that he's gone."

"And the money is gone with him."

"Why is that, Felix?" Murphy asked. "Did you put it in his coffin?"

"No. But what makes you think I have it?" Felix asked.

"We both know where George put the cash, and it ain't there now," Murphy snarled.

"Oh-k, ok, ok," Felix stammered. "About two years ago, when George died, I went to get it out. George was shot, you know that, right?"

"My Money, Felix," a cool Murphy maintained his focus.

"Ok, so George was dead, and I grabbed the money before the cops could find it," Felix said, impatiently.

"And where is my money?!" Murphy demanded.

"Only a third of it was yours."

"Until George died, then *half* of it became mine," Murphy countered with sound logic. "So, where is it?"

"It's gone," Felix confessed after a tense-filled pause.

"*Gone?*" Murphy asked, with his voice calming considerably. Murphy already knew what happened to his money; anyone who had ever known Felix knew exactly what had happened to every dime he ever laid his hands on. "Gone *where?*"

"Listen, Murphy, this job, this other job, you will make it all back and more. We are going to make over twice as much," Felix pleaded, "maybe even three times."

"Felix, *you* are the reason we got caught last time. I am not going back up the river over you," Murphy said. "Now, where is my money? Where did it go?"

Felix stared blankly at Murphy for sometime, thinking hard and fast, trying desperately to think of an angle he could use to talk his way out of this, but after a few moments that seemed to drag on for an eternity, he realized he couldn't think of anything, so he offered Murphy the truth: "I'm sorry, Murph. It … it … I spent it all on powder … powder and ponies."

Murphy leaned back in his chair and went silent. He lifted his coffee mug to his lips and took a long sip. He looked at Felix's beer mug - it was almost empty.

"You got a hole in the bottom of that mug, pal," he said.

Felix looked at his mug to see that there was little more than a couple of sips, or one large gulp, left in his mug. He turned towards the bartender and called out, "Hey! Hey man!"

As the bartender lifted up his head to look, Felix lifted up his mug and waved it at him.

"I need another one, bud!" Felix called out, and then he gulped down the last of his beer.

As Felix was distracted by finishing off his drink, the bartender made eye contact with Murphy, and Murphy nodded.

Putting his empty mug down on the table, Felix said to his table companion: "It's an easy job. You see –"

"No," Murphy interrupted Felix. "I'm not going back, not for *you*."

As Murphy was speaking, the bartender with the teardrop tattoo below his left eye arrived at the table and put a new mug of beer in front of Felix before picking up the empty one. The bartender then walked towards the two men at the pool table while Murphy picked up where he left off.

"You found the last job, and you talked *George* into it, not *me;* I trusted *him*, not you."

Murphy sipped his coffee and darted his eyes towards the pool table. The two men put their cues down and walked sharply, briskly to the door and exited the tavern, while the bartender headed back to the bar.

"It won't be like that this time, Murph. I'll stay straight

until it's over," Felix pleaded. "I need you on this. If I could do it alone, I wouldn't be asking."

"Maybe you should have thought about that before you fucked up and I had to fall on my sword to protect George and my money – all because you needed a fix."

Murphy watched the bartender with the smeared tattoos on his knuckles lean in towards the old man drinking at the bar and whisper something in his ear, then the old man stood up and began to walk to the door and the bartender followed him.

"C'mon, Murph, it wasn't just like *that*."

Felix tried to defend himself, but he could tell it was not going well; Murphy did not seem interested in the job at all. "It is a lot of money," he persisted.

"And you'll blow it all on powder and ponies again," Murphy sneered; in the corner of his eye, he saw the bartender usher the old man out the door, lock it, and nod back to him.

"Well maybe," Felix conceded, "but only my half this

time, Murph, I swear."

Murphy stood up, removed his overcoat from the back of his chair and put it on while looking towards the door and the bartender, whose nod signaled to Murphy that it had been locked.

"Eight years I've been waiting to have a friendly conversation with you, Felix. To put that part of my life behind me."

As he spoke, Murphy began to walk past Felix, who grabbed him by the arm.

"Think about it, Murph, I can't pull this off without you!"

"Goodbye, Felix," Murphy said to his one-time partner, then moved past him to go to the door. Swiftly, suddenly, Murphy pivoted on his feet, squared his body, reached down from behind and snapped Felix's neck, killing him instantly.

Felix's head fell hard onto the table like dead weight, and Murphy stood up tall, and without turning, addressed the bartender.

"You'll get rid of that for me?" Murphy asked, referring to Felix's dead body.

"Yeah. I'll get rid of it for you, Murph," the bartender replied.

"Then we're even for what happened on *the inside*," Murphy said.

As Murphy approached the door, the bartender unlocked it and held it open for him. As Murphy stepped out, the bartender said "Night, Murph" with familiarity.

Murphy stepped out of the tavern and onto the street. He heard the door to the tavern close behind him, and he heard the deadbolt lock.

Murphy stood tall, breathed the crisp, clean, winter air of freedom deep into his lungs, and began to walk away.

ABOUT THE AUTHOR

Jeffrey Kelley is a Canadian author whose titles include *FIVE*, a thriller with Orwellian themes; *A Cathartic Scripture*, a personal story about a man seeking redemption on his own terms; and the book *DISTANCE: Poetry & Critical Essays*.

Jeffrey also wrote the screenplays for *FIVE*, *Frozen Trade*, and *The Gatekeeper*, among others.

In addition to being an author and novelist, Jeffrey is an independent film producer, director and actor.

He also has a dog named Seamus.